The wonderchild within us

Kamraj Sundram

Sarvah League

An art and experience company

Edited by
Steven Ose

Sarvah League

An art and experience company

Dedicated to

my daughter Vasundhara

TABLE OF CONTENTS

Author's Note

Last year, my best friend Easwaramoorthi told me, "The impact you have on my 9-year-old is very telling. Now I understand the work on yourself all these years. I think you can positively contribute to child development initiatives."

I'm not an expert in child education, but I experienced some evidence of his statement from our interactions. His daughter has a continuing impact on me, and I think it is much more than what I believe I have on her.

When I was five years old, my beloved aunt planted a seed in me to cultivate deeper meanings about life and find my purpose. For my entire life and with varying intensities, I have been consciously working on how I interact with myself and others. My life has been filled with failures, successes, struggles, and ultimately is a worthy pursuit.

What more can I do regarding what Easwaramoorthi said? The best thing I have known is sharing what I learned and continue to learn.

****

Since we were kids, haven't we used stories and conversations to learn about the world and find our way?

Does the nature of communication - how and what we communicate - play a role in influencing ourselves and others towards a positive evolution and for generations to come? Just as the moon receives and reflects the light from the sun, we are continually receiving and giving our expressions to each other.

The Indian word 'Guru' means one who dispels darkness. Thus, everyone qualifies as a Guru, as we dispel darkness from each other's lives to whatever possible extent.

Some of us, Gurus, become experts in our chosen field of work. Some of us, experts and others alike, also become closer with each other because of the nature of our relationship.

All these relationships, from at least ten countries in the world where I have lived and visited, enriched my four and a half decades of existence. And they continue to add to the quality of my life.

All these Gurus, i.e., all the people I have met, improved how I interact with myself, and thus, with my sweet daughter, beloved wife, and many others. Such interactions and communications led to the experiential discovery and nurturing of the wonderchild within me.

'The Wonderchild within us' is a collection of my heartfelt thoughts, presented as conversations in imaginative events and stories grounded in real life. My objective is to do my part to improve the interaction within us and with all.

I want to be at your service, dearest parents, parents to be, and our most beloved children.

Thank You,
Kamraj Sundram
04 Jan 2021

Foreword

I feel great joy in introducing this book, "The Wonderchild within us" by *Sri. Kamraj Sundram, whom I fondly address as KKS.

In our life journey from childhood onwards, we interact with various people from different age groups. During these interactions at every stage of our day to day existence, life on this planet inspires us to bring changes within us, our outlook, and influence our surroundings.

We face problems in our everyday lives, some within our control, and some caused by extraneous factors beyond our control. The magnitude of any problem is immaterial since it depends upon each individual, how they view the problem, its actual impact, and the self-induced impact by their approach at that moment.

KKS brings a very humane approach to face situations in our lives. In this book, the author communicates to the reader through various events in families situated across the globe. These families, despite the distance, are still connected through deep friendships with each other. The stories detail events that happen in the lives of this intriguing group of friends and families.

Personally, I learned new ways from how the characters apply their thinking, feeling, and understanding to the events and shape their worldview proactively while contributing positively to people around them. The characters include children capable of thinking on their own, parents, and also grandparents.

The interactions among the family members and friends are on varied subjects, essential and relevant to life and living. Some of the topics covered are love, kindness, character, self-awareness, eating habits, environmental concerns, behavioral tendencies, physical fitness, freedom, responsibility, etc.

The book is also an exciting fiction; it is not pure non-fiction that belongs to the self-help genre. It is a collection of short stories where the key topics are addressed through the characters' experiences and sharing. Each chapter ends with a question for us to ponder about the topic in relation to our own experiences.

I trust the work by KKS appeals to all parents, parents-to-be, and teenagers. The stories are engaging, and they bring a warm and soulful touch with events that I, as a reader, can personally relate based on my life experiences.

I appreciate the tremendous effort by KKS in creating, building characters from all walks of life across the globe, and bringing out 'The wonderchild within us.'

Sincerely,
Ramiah Seshan,
Retd. General Manager (R&D),
TVS Motor Company Limited.

* Sri - a title used to honor a person. The meaning of the word that fits in this context is 'respected.' The deeper meaning is that all life is sacred and has the opportunity to blossom. It is used in India a lot to address any person. It does not mean any stature of a person.

Editor's Note

What an unexpected delight! I met Kamraj Sundram about 17 years ago at a social event. As an American, I was immediately amazed at his level of happiness and excitement - it was an uncommon treat in my experience. In the time I've known him, he has always radiated enthusiasm, joy and a great focus and intensity on learning and growth. Thoughtful and dedicated also describe him well.

My life changed directions, at least geographically, about 5 years ago and we fell out of touch. A lot had shifted for me in the past 5 years and I had become a more serious version of myself, keeping firm to my commitment to provide for my family. When K reached out to me via a popular social media platform to reconnect, it was a welcome break from the intensity of my work life.

And it's been much more than that. As we shared the changes and new events in our lives over the past 5 years, I was impressed to learn he had written a book and was already on his second. Before I could even ask to be on the first list for a copy of the new book, he asked me if I would read and review a chapter. K is, among other things, a feedback enthusiast. He seems to consume feedback like a dessert lover eats apple pie a la mode. I was honored and more than agreeable to have a read.

It's a cliché to say my enjoyment of the content is an understatement, and it's probably even become a cliché to say cliché, but so be it. I quickly fell into my own zone of reading, modifying, suggesting, and inquiring for clarifying points on what he had written. In my life, I would never have expected to be so easily immersed in such a process. The single chapter review and editing lead to an invitation to help with the whole book. It was an easy yes on my part.

K says I am doing a great favor to him for assisting in the editing process while I say he is the one doing a greater favor for giving me first look at what he wants to bring forth. But I know and love that it's a fine team effort, with him in particular, and don't need to compete for the highest favor award.

I am not an editor by profession or training but by passion and involvement in the creative process. I have studied and done my best to apply 'proper writing,' meticulously to honor the strength and beauty language has added to our lives and living. I have done a lot of technical writing, documentation, memos to management and subordinates, and the occasional, annual holiday letter to friends and family. I like to write, read back what I've written, and edit my writing until I produce something that sounds good and hopefully makes sense.

I have endeavored to apply the same process to K's 'The Wonderchild within us,' and hope it makes for a better experience and enjoyment of what he wants to say to the world. And that is substantial; he still has much to say and share, and I believe people can enrich their lives if they become inspired to learn more about what he is working to bring forth. I'm sure the two books only scratch the surface.

If you enjoy his writing, I encourage you to also visit the content he's creating through his company, Sarvah League, website and on YouTube.

Especially coming after the end of a challenging year for many, I wish much joy and peace for all of humanity. Please enjoy the book!

Respectfully,
Steven Ose

Acknowledgments

My sincere thanks to

My beloved spiritual guide and all the previous guides preceding him for gifting me a simple and profound practice of meditation and way of life. All the guides are from India. And the practice has become my lifeline over the years.

Vethathiri Maharishi for helping me understand religion, spirituality, civilization, and a practitioner's responsibility that led me to my guide I mentioned above.

J. Krishnamurti and Viktor Frankl, who live through their work to date and assist my thinking.

'The wonderchild within us' has all the above great beings' presence, expressed directly and otherwise. I am forever grateful to them.

My aunt **Kalyani** who gently kindled an interest to learn about myself from an early age.

Steven Ose, who I met seventeen years ago at a social event. Since that meeting, Steve touches my heart with his sweetness and undying commitment to help. His unasked assistance to pronounce certain words correctly in English, his singing lessons more than a decade ago, and many casual meetings were filled with the beauty and warmth of his personality. He has rendered the necessary edits to this book unreservedly. Along with many other gifts from him, I am also grateful for his work in 'The wonderchild within us.'

Preethi, my wife, the loveliest and kindest soul that I am fortunate to have in my life. Her sharp mind identified logical errors in the book that I overlooked, and her diligence in proofreading provided the essential and necessary quality control.

1

One small step!

The forest smells terrific; the trail and the wind have had exclusive time with each other for countless days. The lone stream along the trail is abundant with fresh and pure water, and the stream hugs all the rocks along its way, creating a symphony. A very few empty soda cans that used to always be present in all the previous hikes are not seen now. Perhaps no one came by after the last clean-up. This is not a usual trail that people frequently hike. Yet, there is a noticeable difference when no one has visited it for the past four months.

Pat walks up the trail while listening attentively, and almost to each and every sound around him. Once in a while, he looks at his watch with amusement. Pat has never taken more than an hour to hike up the trail. It is 8 a.m., already an hour since he started. But he hardly walked one-quarter of the total distance.

A thought crosses his mind that his granddaughter Megan would love the music of the stream. Just like the stream being stopped momentarily by a huge immovable rock, his footsteps slow down and halt at a thought. Many thoughts follow the first one and change his relaxed face to a concerned one. He lets out a deep sigh.

'Why were so many cans and plastic bottles found in the trail previously? Does it take humans to not touch nature to keep the sanctity of nature and the sanity of all life? Aren't we from nature? Aren't our bodies just an extension of nature? And why have we, as a society, become somewhat unnatural?'

Finally, one question stays and deepens its presence in his heart.

"What have we done to the world?"

Approximately 8500 miles away, another person who loves to be in the woods finds himself restricted to a few walls inside his own home.

Naren is silently amused at the situation where he and the rest of the people in the world have locked themselves willingly or reluctantly, but more importantly, by their own volition.

Naren gently closes the lid of his favorite fountain pen.

He does not restrict himself to writing in his journal at a specific daily time. He prefers to be spontaneous as his experiences inspire him throughout each day.

It is time now for a walk on the terrace. Fortunately, Uma, Naren's wife, has chosen a beautiful and friendly neighborhood filled with trees, parrots, and pigeons. During this time of the Covid-19 pandemic, where all movements outside the home are restricted, a visit to the terrace of their apartment complex is heavenly. The birds chirp non-stop, the breeze relaxes them as they walk, and the trees breathe out abundant fresh air.

'Kamali is his life' would be the most appropriate way to describe how Naren feels about his daughter. She is spontaneous, honest, playful, and open-minded.

Kamali is an avid reader, a similarity that she shares with her parents when they were of her age. But her reading rate is way above theirs. She can easily digest 300-400 pages a day while still taking care of her other activities. She tunes in to the character personas so much that she remembers almost everything about them as she reads a book. Sometimes she impersonates the characters, which is entertaining to Naren and Uma.

Kamali has also been taking singing and dance lessons since she was six years old. Now she is thirteen and can perform like a professional dancer and singer.

Naren looks at her lovingly. Kamali is absorbed in her homework. Her focus adds even more beauty to her already beautiful face. Naren releases a deep sigh as a recurring thought finds its way, interrupting his joy.

"What are we giving to our children and to our generations that are yet to come?"

Naren has been asking himself this question for several weeks.

Uma brings her work to a temporary closure, puts her laptop aside, and walks to Naren. She is a talented programmer who also loves programming. In fact, she has refused several offers for higher management roles within the organization for which she works. Accepting such roles would mean she would have less time for what she loves.

Uma learned to sing when she was five. When she is happy, she sings. When she is in sorrow, she sings. She sings when she is excited. Basically, she loves to sing for any mood. She is the foundation of their lovely family of three.

The evening sun withdraws its rays. Naren, Kamali, and Uma ease their walk to the terrace of their apartment complex. The sun will set in twenty minutes. The orange-hue sky, the contrasting green leaves of the trees that are taller than their apartment complex, and the birds' greeting evoke great joy in them.

"Uma! I see more parrots than earlier. Is that right?"

"No, Naren. I think you are imagining. It is true for many other places, but not here. Our neighborhood is always parrot friendly."

Naren agrees with Uma, the more observant of the three of them. Uma's melodious voice fills the air, and further relaxes him. Uma is singing, while Kamali is jumping around, being fully immersed in her world.

Naren's thoughts go to his friend. "Pat must be walking up the trail about now," he tells Kamali.

Kamali exclaims, "Dad! I wish we could join him!"

"I know, Kamali. I do too. I was telling your mother that we all could visit Pat next summer. I'm not sure when air travel will open. And when it does, I wonder whether traveling will become as enjoyable as it used to be.

We may not be talking with our next seat neighbors. We would be worried about our masks, sanitizers, and those who do not maintain social distance. That is no fun."

Uma says, "People are resilient, but it will take time for some things in life to return to as we knew. Even then, it will never be as it was before."

"At least the birds won't collide with the planes." Kamali spurts her words as she dances around.

"She is right," thinks Naren.

Naren recently heard there have been reports of rare animals and sea-life sighted for the first time. It's apparently due to people staying home, fearing the Covid-19 pandemic. The year is 2020. Naren thinks about how our ancestors might have handled the Spanish flu outbreak a century ago. The communities and countries then were less connected, and they did not have the advanced medical care and technology of today for their assistance.

About 50 million people died then, according to the United States Centers for Disease Control and Prevention.

'We are better off compared to the struggle and pain of our ancestors, relatively speaking. But sadly, we could not avoid deaths altogether.'

At the same time, Naren is optimistic, and he maintains an enthusiastic and hopeful view of life. In a few hours he is going to call Pat.

He immerses in a different thought.

'How would transcontinental communication, talking great distances across the oceans, be possible without the technological achievements humanity has made?'

They come home when it is time to prepare for dinner. Uma plays chef, with Naren as her assistant. Kamali also helps them with simple tasks. Thanks to the committed grocery workers who deliver at home, they never lack food in their cupboards.

***

Pat completes his walk on the trail, thinks of lighting up a cigar, but decides against it. Pat gave up smoking three years ago. Every now and then, the desire for nicotine attempts to find its way but fails against his strong will. His hands carry the plants' fragrance from alongside the trail, and he decides not to wash it away.

After preparing a cup of coffee, he sets aside the collection of beautiful, fallen flowers that he brought back from his trail walk, places them on the long, empty dining table, and moves to the couch.

Skype's ring tone sings from his computer. It is Naren, calling from India.

"Citizen of the World! How are you?"

Pat always likes to call Naren' Citizen'. He says since Naren has traveled to so many parts of the world, he thinks it is appropriate, and he is fit to be called a Citizen of the World, or just Citizen.

"Gandalf! I am well, and how have you been?"

For Naren, Pat is always Gandalf from the Lord of the Rings, a beloved friend, a dear elder brother, and a wise mentor. Pat doesn't like the 'old' trait of Gandalf, but he never says anything to Naren, as he knows what's in his friend's heart.

"It's been just a couple of days since we spoke. I am good as I was. Since then, the only news is that I postponed paying my bills as I can't afford them right now."

"I am sorry to hear that. You will find a way soon, Pat." Naren has a genuine concern for Pat.

"You said you were going to the trail. How was it?"

Naren loves to hear Pat speak about the trail. Last summer, when Naren visited Pat, they hiked up and discovered a shared enthusiasm for the woods and conversing along their walk.

Pat says that he spent six hours on the trail today. Naren is surprised and elated! Pat continues to share happily.

"It was incredible! I had no other thoughts pulling me here or there. I felt completely present and savored every bit of my walk. Thank you for showing me those meditation sessions, Citizen. They were so helpful!"

"I am glad, Pat. I thank my aunt and other lovely teachers from India who persisted for decades to improve my meditation. I don't have the luxury of just stepping into the woods and disappear these days, as I live in a crowded city.

Yet, we go to the beach and spend hours walking and sitting on the sand whenever we can. Before the pandemic, we were regularly visiting the beach on full moon days. My last visits were memorable. I had almost no thoughts and was fully attentive to the endless beauty in front of me.

Although from time to time lately, I'm very sad about a contradiction, I observe more and more in front of my eyes."

"What is it?"

"Well, for example. I am talking to you with this small black thing, my mobile phone, and am sitting several thousand miles away. I'm very happy that technology is so advanced. People have also learned how to mass-produce goods and tools and make them affordable for many others. Yet our manufacturing practices are wreaking havoc in the world."

"How so?"

"Look! We have been in lockdown for just about a month. We heard the news in India that many unseen animals visit our villages and even city roads. We heard that sea-life thrives better now.

Air pollution has drastically reduced in one of our urban cities where people used to wear a mask. Now they wear a mask for Covid but can see the blue sky and count the stars at night.

The lungs of our children are given a welcome break from bad air. Why didn't we see and experience such results before the pandemic? It's because we were driving our cars, buses, and bikes going everywhere and anywhere.

Freighters were moving goods we needed, as well as the ones we didn't. It is most often the goods that we didn't need that ruled our roadways.

Imprison humanity! Other lives thrive now! Isn't that how it's become?"

"So, you think our manufacturing practices are bad, huh?"

"Not as much on the technique. But the reasons why we manufacture so much that is not used. We produce food that can take care of feeding ten billion people, yet so much is wasted and many people still die of hunger.

We make gadgets and sell them to the same population who can afford them year after year when there is no need. A lot of waste materials we create are not biodegradable. I can go on."

"When we begin to critically evaluate why we think we need something, how much of it, and at what cost things are produced, it will change."

"I agree, Pat. The challenge is that we maintain a culture and societal habits that inhibit critical thinking. Let me share with you a cute and yet sad example. It's an incident from my own life about two years ago. When I got back to my writing after an errand, Kamali smiled and said that she had typed something on my laptop.

'Juice eating monster comes into town. Princess Alli saves the baby unicorn and teaches the monster how to be kind. So, the beast becomes good. THE END.'

'TIP: Monsters love juice, so give it to them before you teach them, and they will become good monsters.'

Our kids are taught if we give what someone wants, the person will stop their bad behavior and start doing good. We shape the children to be compliant to the people, elders, teachers, and almost anyone in the name of civil behavior. Then at some point, the children who are now adults rebel against those teachings and rules.

And what is the result? Most of us of today either comply or rebel and think less. Defiance to a rule is not the same as thinking and coming up with holistic solutions.

If such is our training, how will we learn to evaluate and decide whether our actions will wreak havoc for others? I'm not saying no one evaluates. It's just the proportion of those who don't is far greater than those who do."

"Citizen, I agree with you. Unfortunately, we blame more than we think. Some blame technology for today's problems and some blame our consumption. However, a society that is afraid to spend is also a society that is afraid to advance. Nowadays, I see angry kids in social media ridiculing technology, probably trained by their equally angry parents, while using an incredible technological invention, the internet, to do so.

This is blame and harmful. If we want to make our technology holistic and improve our conduct around consumption, anger and blame alone will not help.

It is in our interest to buy products and services that fuel further inventions and advance the quality of human life. And it's necessary to find a balance between production and consumption. Blaming the cause of all problems entirely on technology or our consumption leads to nothing but a dead end."

Kamali is keenly listening to Pat and Naren. Uma also joins them.

"Uncle Pat! Do you know any company that manufactures without concern for others?"

"Oh, I can call out so many, Kamali. A few decades ago, there was a company that used to make clothes in our town. They didn't want to spend money on the proper disposal of their wastewater. They just piped it all into a river that runs close to our town. They also conveniently built their plant just next to the river. Spending money on proper disposal of wastewater would increase their cost, and they would not be able to compete with others on price.

But they marketed themselves as the company that cares for blue-collar workers getting access to quality clothes at an affordable price.

They were quite successful until an honest mayor took action against them. A dog that accidentally jumped in the river one day developed a skin disease. Upon finding the source of its infection, the dog's owner promptly brought the issue to the mayor's office. It was fortunate that it became a warning sign for people who avoided getting into the water.

The mayor took swift actions and had the company shut its operations. She worked with the court and other authorities and revoked the license of the company to do business."

"Did the company ask for forgiveness from the community?" Kamali is curious.

"No, and that's a shame! Instead, they opened a business under another name and resumed product manufacturing in an Asian country.

A local reporter followed up on the company's practices, and he dared travel to that country to observe. The reporter found similar practices and effects on people in the previous neighborhood to the new business location in the foreign country. He was saddened to learn that most companies perform such thoughtless acts of production, ruining the developing country's natural resources and air quality. He returned to the States and wrote a bold article.

At least in our town, most people vowed not to support and purchase the cloth manufacturer's imports. But legally, no local action could be taken against them. They have since grown and become a large, international apparel maker."

Uma speaks, "That is so sad! If everyone in the country had taken your town's stance, that company could have been stopped."

Naren adds, "I know this company, too. They also have a members' club and entice people through marketing, sales, and promotions to buy clothes for every occasion – family events, reunions, and all the national holidays. They offer their products dirt cheap, and most of the loyal customers regularly buy more clothes than they need. The company had the gall to broadcast a promotional video showing a working-class woman's room in a house. The room was filled with at least a couple hundred articles of clothing and nothing else. They were all nicely organized in large wardrobes. The advertisement was titled, 'You can live rich even if you are blue-collar. You deserve it!'

I was shocked that the company was cultivating thoughtless spending behavior and was also convincing people that their economic status made them deserve things."

Uma asks a question. "How does a person conclude that what he or she has is enough? And how does he or she stop when they know the answer?"

Pat asks, "Well, Kamali! Maybe you can answer this one! We, adults, are badly failing at this question. How do you know how much to consume such that it does not affect other things and people in an adverse way?"

"I'm not sure. For me, I just stop eating as soon as my stomach is full. I don't like how it feels to overeat."

The adults know not to overeat, but only as an idea. To hear from Kamali, an honest answer to how she handles food appeals directly to their hearts. All three adults feel moved at the simplicity of Kamali's response, which also contains a crucial part of the solution. Before thinking about the impact on everyone else, does each person think about the implications for themself? If they don't or can't, how could they feel deeply about the effects on others?

Pat talks to Kamali and the others.

"Kiddo! I love what you said! Most of the world likes to overeat, and sure we often eat more than our bodies need when we become somewhat wealthy since we can afford to do so. We overeat not just our food, but everything.

And those of us who eat just a little more justify that it does not count as it is only a tiny little more than what is required. Or we convince ourselves that it is a small weakness, negligible, and sometimes is an essential distraction but keep doing it all the time, not just sometimes.

There are many other aspects to the production systems and processes that we cannot easily find about the things we consume, such as where they are made? How they are made? Did the manufacturing process adversely affect people's lives? And more!

But if we just stop over-consuming beyond what we need, maybe that will systemically affect all the other things, starting with overproduction for one group at another's expense.

It doesn't mean that you can't enjoy an ice cream just because you can live without it, but you don't have to overindulge and eat bowl after bowl in one sitting.

Following what your dad said, if we stop getting angry at and blaming each other for the problems, then we can start to look together at the solutions and learn to treat each other with kindness while still holding people accountable. It's easier said than done, but is so worthwhile to make the attempt."

Kamali is listening to Pat while seating her 'Clifford, the Dog' toy. It is the same old toy that she got as a gift when she was five.

She refuses to buy or accept new toys until her old ones are worn out and unusable. When that time comes, she sends the worn-out toys for recycling, after a sad farewell.

Uma and Naren look at each other and feel proud of their conscientious and graceful daughter.

Kamali always questions when Naren buys the biggest loaf of bread or a big bottle of jam. She understands that a bigger thing is necessary at times but still questions her parents' purchases.

So Naren learns to buy things in adequate quantity and lovingly explains to Kamali why the larger size is sometimes needed.

"You know something, Gandalf. Whenever we get Kamali a chocolate bar, she savors it and sometimes keeps it for weeks or even months."

"No surprise there," chuckles Pat. "That's my girl."

"Uncle Pat! Please tell me about the trail. How was it?"

"Look, Citizen! Your daughter calls me 'Uncle.' Maybe you should think twice before calling me Gandalf. It would seem I am still very young!"

Pat and Naren laugh together.

Pat begins to speak about the trail, the symphony of the stream, the fresh smell of the blossoming trees, and above all, his forgetfulness of any worries and being there, one with the trail. Kamali listens attentively and asks him questions. Uma and Naren watch Pat and Kamali, with full feelings of warmth and affection.

Can small actions yield big results?

2

When was the last time you saw a snake?

It is not an easy month. Acquiring new clients was already difficult. With so much community, regional, and world focus on safeguarding against the pandemic, finding new businesses has become exponentially more challenging.

Clark, a man who has endured many challenges in his career, looks at the early morning sky. It's been a long while since he spent so much time in his wife's agriculture fields. The wet soil massages his feet while the freshness of the running water, pumped from the ground well, partners with the rice crops to dance gleefully with the wind.

Clark came to India sixteen years ago to expand his business offshore. He sometimes reflects how the business plan didn't foresee how he would fall in love with the country; and with Kavya. In the early days of his visit, Clark did not hesitate to engage in food adventures.

The consequence of his unintended indulgence led him to the hospital where Kavya worked as a house-surgeon, a role in her final year of education. It was love at first sight for Clark, and perhaps at fifth or sixth sight for Kavya. And now Clark and Kavya have been happily married for fifteen years.

Neha comes running. "Dad! Kamali, Aunty Uma and Uncle Naren are on their way."

Neha's excitement is tangible, and Clark sheds off his blues as soon as he hears her. Kavya and Uma are schoolmates, and over the years, Naren has become one of Clark's dear friends.

Clark does not have any siblings, and he grew up alone as a child for the most part. In his early days in India, Clark felt odd as most women younger than him called him 'brother,' and children called him 'Uncle.' When he understood how genuinely they personalized relationships, he humbly accepted being an Uncle and a brother.

Uma gradually took a place in his heart as he imagined a close sister might. Kamali has impressed Clark as the most compassionate child he has ever met. He experienced the resemblance when he learned that 'Kamali' means one who has a beautiful face and characteristics of the lotus plant. Lotus has been used in countless metaphors in poetry and spirituality in India. Clark recalls:

"A life best lived is when you can be like the lotus leaves on which the water drops sit as they are. You can be that way with all the relationships in your life – people and things – with whom you interact.

When you do not allow those relationships to have a hold on your emotions, just as how the lotus leaves accept but are unencumbered by the water, you live joyfully; free of worry and fear."

"How could one not worry about money?" Clark ponders in contradiction to what he admires about the lotus leaves. "How can you move anything in the world without money?"

"Yes," his inner dialog continues. "But why do you fear losing what you do and do not have? If a time comes when you have no money at all, you will either deal with it or perish. Why fear now?"

The mature thoughts of his mind ridicule the not so mature ones. It is as if the deep sea forgets that the waves are its extensions and ridicules why the waves are restless.

Clark feels the conflict as his thoughts wrestle each other for their point of view to prevail. One set predicts an impending doom, betraying his rational mind and inspiring a deep sense of fear, and the other set judges him as a weak person for feeling that way.

"Who thinks this way? It's as if there are two independent people inside me." Clark chuckles. Thanks to a few honest friends, he is aware that he is not the only one who has such a tug of war between his schools of thought.

"When will they be here, Neha?"

"Anytime in the next ten to fifteen minutes." Neha keeps jumping in joy. She loves Naren and Uma, who play and talk with her tirelessly. And she has so much fun talking with Kamali, who knows every event in the Harry Potter series of books.

Clark can openly speak to Naren about how he actually feels when he is troubled about things. He doesn't have to pretend and act like a man who has it 'all together.' He is looking forward to talking with Naren about his worries over money.

Clark and Neha walk back to the farmhouse. Clark walks briskly to try and keep up with Neha, who is running. In a while, he starts running to catch up with her. Clark notices that Neha does not pay attention to the rough surface beneath her bare feet. When he realizes there is nothing on the ground that could actually hurt her, he stops worrying and engages in a playful race with Neha to be the first one to the house.

Naren, Uma, and Kamali arrive.

After exchanging greetings, the two families sit at the dining table to enjoy lunch. Kavya has made a sumptuous feast. She is a great host and an affectionate friend who considers everyone as her family.

Clark notices Naren is spending a lot of time chewing his food.

"Naren! What's going on?"

Kamali jumps in. "He is chewing each bite forty times."

"Really? Why?"

"Clark! I watched an excellent speech by the actor R. Madhavan, titled 'Drink your food, chew your water.' When I heard the video title, I ignored it for two months as it felt tasteless.

During the two months, though, I noticed that I was eating food faster and faster, as I felt restless. The hotter the weather and the sweatier my body became, the more restless I was while eating.

I would finish my meals in next to no time while Uma and Kamali were still eating. I did not like that!"

"So, you started chewing each bite forty times so that you can eat along with them?"

"He-he! Well, it was the motivation to finally watch the video.

After watching it, I discovered it's not about a liquid diet as I imagined. I wanted the benefits they revealed, so I started to follow the suggestions. Let me explain.

Let's say a car factory is on an important deadline to deliver 100 cars, no matter what. Management communicates the mandate clearly to all teams. The assembly line starts moving, and the employees go about their tasks. One team hangs the doors, another one mounts the tires, another installs the engines, etc.

The various parts pass through the busy hands of each team to finally emerge as a car. Now suppose if the first group does the job haphazardly, after which they are absent from their section? The next group of people, who do not have the expertise or the right equipment, would need to fix the job or perform the prior set of tasks with what they have, then move on. They cannot delay completion and must honor the deadline.

Similarly, our intestines can't afford to wait. They don't have any teeth to grind the food, a task which should have been performed by another 'team,' yet they take up the tedious and tiresome job of moving the food down the line. So, many side effects, such as feeling sluggish, unmotivated, and falling ill, begin to crop up.

Additionally, when I pay attention to chewing my food well, I have noticed I talk less during the meal and feel very peaceful. My mind has one simple, gentle focus, and I almost don't worry about anything."

"Well, I don't like how all the different food items taste the same after you chew it forty times," Uma says.

"Uma, you get to enjoy the taste in the first few bites. For me, that is enough," smiles Naren.

"Okay, okay. I will do twenty, and that is plenty," Kamali laughs.

"Naren! I can't afford to spend that much time eating," says Clark.

"Well, you would end up eating a healthy quantity and become more focused. Isn't that a better trade-off than gulping food away, like you're racing to a finish line, only to not win and feel exhausted?"

"I agree with Madhavan and you, dear brother. Shall we enjoy the food and sit under the coconut trees and talk all we want? How about that?" Kavya says.

Everyone nods in agreement and focuses on eating. They have nothing but praises for Kavya's cooking. By the time they finish savoring the delicious meal, the sun's intensity has diminished some, so they all stroll to a hut located between the coconut trees.

The energetic Neha and Kamali run to the Mango trees and start climbing.

"What is bothering you, Clark?"

"The usual thing, Naren. I worry about the future of our business. I'm not sure whether it can get us even half the money we earned last year."

"I understand. I have the same concern. And this worrying is a tricky business. Have we not worried when our businesses were doing well?"

"Hmm. We have. However, the worry and fear about money are more intense than about anything else. It unsettles me."

"Yes, brother! I feel that way too," says Kavya.

"Welcome to the club," says Uma.

"I know. I feel that way as well," says Naren.

"Why is it so bothersome when we think we will earn less than last year? We have enough right now to provide for ourselves and cover expenses for at least three years. Still, the moment we think about even the possibility of the money decreasing each year, it feels very unsettling," shares Clark.

"Since our childhood, we are instilled with a fear of survival related to earning money. We were frightened by so many stories of what happened to people who were financially poor. Even as adults, we continue the same pattern of getting scared and feeling unable to think. It's funny that when I experience the fears related to money as a grown man, my thoughts still descend to a dark place.

Of course, this is in direct contradiction to all the teachings in our culture, since time immemorial, that we can choose what we want to think, feel, and do. So in theory, we know why we feel what we feel, and we know we have a choice to feel. But in our day to day reality, we don't."

Neha and Kamali are running very fast towards them, their faces panic-stricken. "Snake! Snake!"

The mothers bring them quickly inside the house. Clark and Naren run to the Mango tree where their daughters were playing, only to see the Snake's track through the leaves. Clark does not kill the snakes. He has a way of leading them far outside the fields and into the jungle. They were too late this time and could not find the Snake. So, they end the search and go back to the house.

The kids are calm and look relaxed. They are narrating how fast the Snake slithered towards them. Their eyes grow large as they re-live the moment. Clark and Naren watch them for a while, then go to wash their hands and feet. Naren proceeds to the kitchen to make tea for everyone.

Clark continues the conversation from where they left off.

"I am not able to do everything I know. In such cases, I feel as though I'm on a speeding wagon, going downhill where the emotions take my thoughts. We watch ourselves doing the same thing, almost helplessly. Isn't it?"

Uma shares, "I recently read a book called "Man's search for meaning" by Viktor Frankl. Using what I gathered from the book, I think our will is strengthened by the meaning we give to life. I believe with a strong will, we can do what we know."

"Is the meaning we give to our life not a far larger topic than how to not feel unsettled, even though we know we can afford to get by for three years"? Clark asks.

"Not really." Naren walks from the kitchen with a tray and serves the tea to all of them. "Isn't it our perspective on the subject that determines our minds' tendencies - their thoughts and how we feel? We feel unsettled because of how we view things in life. For example, a snake charmer loves to see and play with a snake, whereas we run for our lives.

The snake charmer would have had the first experience with a snake, at which point he had no experience or skill to handle it, right? There was something about him where he had an interest in playing with the snake, as opposed to us who want to avoid snakes at all cost. Two different outlooks and two different outcomes!"

"Hmm. What is my outlook on life, then?" Clark is pensive.

Naren speaks further. "Our outlook on life – I like that question, Clark! I am with you. First, understand, we did not learn to practice enough to develop our outlook on life, character, and attitude in school or in our families.

Most of our schooling was about learning tools to earn money and make a living, deeply motivated by a fear of survival. It's an exaggerated sense of survival, obviously, and should not be what we pass down to our children."

Clark shares. "It seems our current outlook on life is a mixture of many things, but ultimately and fundamentally mixed with fear. It drives the question of 'What will happen to me and those close to me if things are not as I expect?'

When all we imagine is the worst-case scenario, layered by our fear, anxiety, and frustration, there is no space for clarity. This type of imagination weighs down our inner self. It seems there is no other choice in those moments."

Neha and Kamali are listening to the conversation attentively. Neha turns to Kavya.

"I'm always afraid of my exams.

If I eat before I go to the exam hall, I either shove the food down my throat really fast or don't want to eat."

"I know, my dear!" Kavya holds Neha's hands. Turning to the adults, Kavya continues, "Perfect love removes fear. I heard my friend quote that from the bible. As Viktor Frankl said, the meaning we place on people and things we come across each moment could deepen our love. With that understanding, we can change our outlook on life."

"And we can chew the food with love forty times." Kamali giggles.

All the adults look at Neha and Kamali lovingly. The kids sometimes amaze them with their capacity to pay attention and say things that might seem out of context at first, but actually is not.

"Fear is essential also, isn't it? Without it, our kids would not have saved themselves from the snake." Uma speaks.

"Yes, as the situation actually warrants. How many times in a day does snake come toward us? Or some other animal, or even a violent person? When we are afraid, we're not able to think about anything but to save ourselves. That is the nature of fear, an emotion associated with the primitive brain, also referred to as our lizard brain.

That would explain why when we're afraid, we are unable to do higher brain functions such as reflection or contemplation." Kavya brings her knowledge as a doctor and a therapist to the discussion.

"That is why practicing and being able to pause a strong emotion like fear is important. Only after we have developed that discipline can we think better and address the situation. Viktor Frankl says, *'Between stimulus and response there is a space. In that space is our power to choose our response. In our response lies our growth and our freedom,'* Uma contributes.

"The problem is the moment I feel fear, I have thoughts that judge me as weak and illogical for feeling scared." Clark shares.

Naren responds, "Boys should not be afraid. Boys should not cry. Isn't that what we were taught? Why would we not judge ourselves at the self-admittance that we *are* afraid and *want* to cry? It's an absurd tradition, but we still keep such ancient teachings without examination, and continue handing them down to our future generations."

"We have so many psychological habits that are unconscious, accepted, and reinforced throughout our lives, which keep us from recognizing we can pause at any given time. If we practice stillness, in the face of any event - real or imaginary - then we can begin to discover a different choice is possible, a different emotion, a different thought, a different action." Kavya speaks passionately.

"Yes. This makes sense to me.

We need to do homework even more than our children. Being able to pause will allow me to see how I treat myself for feeling afraid. I can stop judging myself as weak," said Clark.

"Yes. And an opportunity to shape our outlook on life to what we want it to be. Then we will only fear actual snakes. We will not fear the sticks, mistaking them for snakes, and we will not spend time worrying that snakes will arrive later to bite me." Uma completes her thoughts with her snake metaphor.

Naren jumps from where he is sitting and exclaims, "Snake! Snake!"

Everyone jumps and runs to whatever place they think is safe, only to find Naren just standing where he was with a smile. They understand he fooled them and rush to him. He runs away from them as they all give chase. The chorus of their laughter gives the air a gregarious human touch.

Is it possible to not worry?

3

Catch me if you can!

Pat wakes up before sunrise. He likes his coffee black, and he always sets the timer on his coffee maker such that the coffee is ready when he wakes up.

Conscious of his aging muscles, Pat stretches his body as his second task of the day. The first thing he does is looking at the photo of his two granddaughters and grandson, and sits in sincere prayer for their wellbeing. Pat does not pray to a specific anthropomorphic god. He prays to the force which holds the universe together. And he believes this force is 'Love' in the human context.

Since his conversation with Kamali and her parents, Pat stopped overeating. He is conscious of all his spending, his words, his money, and even his thoughts.

Pat sits by the huge window, which takes almost all of the wall in the living room when he enjoys his coffee. He designed the window so that he can look at the trees, grass, and the rest of nature.

After his morning coffee, Pat writes in his journal. "*An ounce of practice is worth more than tons of preaching - by Mahatma Gandhi*. And thanks to dearest Kamali for reminding me of this truth."

"The so-called minor deviations of ours that we consider okay are how we excuse ourselves away from the greatness that comes from exercising responsibility in every choice."

At the same time, Pat is sensible. He is not hard on himself for having overeaten by a bite or two.

Pat picks up the beautiful basket of ripe tomatoes left by the door. The tomatoes are from his neighbors.

He chuckles, thinking, "I'm not an old man."

Since the pandemic spread this year, Pat started bringing some vegetables and food to an elderly woman's doorstep in his neighborhood. She is in her late eighties. Pat always leaves the basket by the door.

On the very first day of his loving act, he found a bag of vegetables and nicely packed cooked food at his doorstep. It was left by a neighbor.

"I am just getting to 60, not old yet." Pat smiles.

At the same time, he felt a deepening faith in humanity. He does not know who among his neighbors has left him the vegetables and food. Similarly, the elderly woman also does not know that it's Pat who leaves the vegetables for her.

He makes a breakfast sandwich while wishing his family was with him now. There has been no movement in and out of town for the past three months. Despite his product's slow sales, he keeps himself engaged by making creative and useful things of wood. He has his own sawmill, and he only brings fallen trees to make the products. He doesn't fell any live trees.

The sun is out and about. It is 6:30 p.m. in India. Perhaps he can show Kamali around the property and his workshop. Pat calls Naren on WhatsApp. In no time, Kamali is journeying with him to the beaver dam behind Pat's home, his garden of vegetables, and finally, Pat's lovely wood workshop.

Pat lifts a piece hidden in a velvet cloth.

"Dearest! When you visit me next year, you can hold this in person." And he unwraps the piece.

"Aww! Such a lovely doggie!" Kamali has a soft side for dogs. "What lovely woodwork, Uncle Pat!" She exclaims in joy.

Pat feels delighted to witness her enjoyment. He asks, "So, what have you been up to?"

"Well, I have lots of homework, but no classes. I watch some videos on the phone and do my worksheets. Dad and Mom are busy until 6:30 in the evening. Both showed me a way to organize my time and do the things I like. I practice dancing and singing a bit, and also watch my favorite show for an hour. After 6:30, we have our family time."

"Very nice. It seems you have a pretty good schedule."

"I miss my BFFs, though."

"Let me guess what that means. Your Best Friends Forever?"

"Yes, they both are in different towns, and we are only able to talk on the phone."

"That's too bad. I am sorry, Kamali. You know I miss my granddaughter too."

"Hmm…"

"Well, you asked me one day about how I was at a young age. Do you want to hear now?"

"YES."

Kamali is so happy. She always likes to listen to stories.

Pat travels in his memories. His eyes that are wet for a moment, come back to shower the same kindness that he always shares with Kamali.

"I was the only boy in my family, and I had a sister, four years younger than me. We all, friends and family, and the whole town, loved her so much. While I was always like a wild animal, running around, breaking things, and always active, she brought the family many calm moments of happiness. Her name is Angela. The name means 'messenger of God.' She sure was. Whenever my father came home after a day's work, he would express nothing but happiness at the sight of Angela. He would instantly change any anger or frustration he had at the sight of her smile.

My sister and I, along with cousins and friends from the neighborhood used to play in the evenings. We boys did not usually include the girls because of all the injuries we'd get while playing football or baseball. But we made an exception for Angela. She was not as strong physically as we were, but she was just as spirited. She would run hard, fight hard, and wouldn't mind the occasional wound. Still, we would stop all play if she got injured. She didn't like the special treatment at first. She fought with us often that we considered her weak. She eventually gave in to our wishes and habits. She began to enjoy special treatment. And she did not stop playing hard.

My childhood days from age five to ten were filled with moments of play, happiness, and sharing. When I was eleven, things started to change in my family. My father and mother were becoming less tolerant of each other's habits. We began to see them fight over certain things.

They would stop their arguments, though, as soon as they noticed Angela. The times I sensed a dispute between them was about to start, I would take Angela out of the house and get her an ice cream. I always had some money with me, as I started doing simple jobs, like babysitting for neighbors, working a few hours at the cash register of a nearby gas station, or walking the dog of a blind neighbor.

Whenever Angela would question about the fight between my parents, I would not tell her any details that I already knew. I would change the topic. I thought I should protect her from feeling unhappy and sad. After nagging me for some time, she would stop asking questions. This went on for two years.

Thanks to my friends, I still had a great life outside my home. And inside my home, Angela filled my longing for warmth, affection, and friendship as I fulfilled hers.

In two years, except for one of my best friends, everyone left the town, as their fathers or mothers found better work opportunities. I felt somewhat alone and started looking for new friends.

That's when I met Robert, who was called Fun Bob by his friends. Fun Bob did pranks almost all the time, smoked cigarettes in style, and had a gang. I thought it was cool. He also was the tallest thirteen-year-old I have ever met, besides myself. After I proved I could knock down the strongest boy in his gang, he included me. I was able to do it after two failed attempts, though. In those failed attempts, I returned home with bruises and wounds. Angela made me forget those in no time.

When she asked me how I got them, I lied that they were from a bike ride. Angela knew that I used to ride my bike very fast. She didn't have the kind of experience I had to differentiate an injury from a fall, versus another from a fight. We took care of her all the time and made sure that she did not struggle with any injury. However, there were a few, but hardly anything serious.

Father and mother, despite fights between them, always spoke to Angela affectionately. One day, when I returned home after school, I saw Angela with two boys at a distant corner of my street. Something felt odd, and I ran to them. I beat both the boys to a pulp after I found that they were bullying her. She was already in shock at hearing harsher words and feeling the anger from the boys. And she couldn't stomach my violence against the boys.

When I finished with the boys and turned to her, I found her on the ground, fainted. I lifted her in my hands and ran to the nearby hospital. That was the first day I prayed after many years. I did so only for Angela. She woke up as I walked into the doctor's room with her. I choked up words from my throat and told the doctor whatever I could. The doctor did a system check briefly and assured us that it was a simple response to her experiencing the violence, and there was no problem. I did not believe it until Angela smiled at me.

We both came home. I picked up two slices of pizza from Angela's favorite restaurant on the way. I fed her as soon as we got back and comforted her to sleep. When my father and mother came home after work, I brought them to the study room and explained what happened.

I warned them that if they would not stop fighting in the house, I would walk out of the house with Angela. They both assured me that they would never fight in the home again.

There was something special about Angela. I thought that almost everyone was warm and friendly with her and helped her. This was true with her classmates, especially the male ones. She was the prettiest and the kindest girl I have ever seen in my life. She never developed any contempt towards other girls based on beauty. She did not push away any boy also because he looked ugly or weak or not smart. She was a good student and a sincere friend."

"Uncle Pat! Why are you speaking in the past tense?"

Pat's eyes become moist.

"She is no more, dear. And that is part of the story."

Kamali's eyes also become moist instantly. She is an empathetic child. She feels deeply sad for Angela, who she would never meet in life.

"I'm sorry, Uncle Pat. If you feel very sad, you can tell me the story some other day."

"Kamali, thank you!

I'm fine. We can continue. Where was I?"

"You said Angela was a good student and a sincere friend."

"Yes, yes. And always helped by all of us for anything and everything. Opening doors for Angela, carrying her school bag, sometimes carrying her, always anticipating what might happen to her, catching her before she fell." Pat repeats the last phrase again, "Catching her before she fell."

"My parents eventually divorced when I was fifteen, and we both stayed at my mother's after then. At the same time my friendship with Fun Bob grew deeper and deeper.

I respected Bob as he never bullied a girl, never spoke bad about any girl, and always acted like a gentleman with a girl or woman. Sometimes I brought my sister along with me when we met. Everyone acted politely, served her food or drinks, whatever they were having and treated her well.

My sister also liked Fun Bob, but she didn't particularly like the ones who were overly aggressive, in words or in action. Fun Bob noticed this, and whenever we spent time together with my sister, he made sure there were only friends my sister liked or did not react adversely to.

I was twenty, and Angela was seventeen. She wanted to have a beer that night when we went out with Fun Bob. After a lot of deliberation, I allowed her. As she never had any alcohol until then, in a few sips, she was intoxicated. I urged Bob that we should leave, and he promptly agreed. Angela and I were in the back seat of the jeep, which didn't have any doors.

Against my protest, Angela would not put on her seat belt. She was sometimes dancing, and otherwise talking nonstop. In a bit, I heard her screaming. "I am falling, Pat," I caught her in no time and pulled her inside. My heartbeat was up the charts while I found Angela laughing.

I understood she did a prank with me, not a fun one for me, though. Fun Bob joined her in laughter, and I got angry at both of them. "Never do that again, alright?" I grunted.

We stopped at a familiar gas station and were promptly warned by the attendant that there were cops farther ahead. I knew if they pulled us over with Bob driving, we would be in trouble. I was the only one who was hardly drunk because I stopped after a couple of sips. As I noticed Angela getting intoxicated in a few sips, I stopped my drinking and paid attention to her. So, we decided that I would drive. Fun Bob joined Angela in the back seat. We were indeed stopped by the cops who were doing a 'drunk driver test,' I easily passed the test. They let us go but warned us to sit tight and keep our seatbelts on, even for the back-seat riders as the jeep had no doors. I resumed driving.

"Bob, I'm falling!" Angela screamed, and Bob caught her just as I did the last time. Bob and Angela laughed so hard while I was so mad. I asked Angela to stop playing. She did not. And Bob played along with her, catching her all the time, though he was quite drunk. Angela stopped playing the 'falling prank' and fell asleep.

I was enjoying the quiet ride and noticed that Fun Bob also passed out. Then suddenly, I heard her scream, but with her laughter, "I am falling." I turned back to see that she had actually fallen. Bob was asleep. I slammed the brake so hard. I ran to her and found my Angela breathless, lying by the road. That was the last time I heard her laugh.

Bob was shaken so much that he stopped everything he used to do. I was not myself for years. I cursed myself those years for agreeing to let her drink. I didn't want to talk to any of my family and moved away from my town. I stopped answering any calls from my parents and my grandmother, who lived in Texas. Three years after this unfortunate incident, somehow, I finally decided to answer when my grandmother called. I cried with her that I killed Angela, and it was such a bad idea that I allowed her to drink the beer. My grandmother heard me patiently. In her kindest voice she told me that many others, including my parents, including herself, Angela, and I made mistakes that led to her death. She comforted me that those mistakes were out of love and lack of knowledge. I asked her what my mistake was.

She said, "We all prevented her from taking care of simple things in life. Carrying her stuff, catching her while playing so that she does not fall, not letting sad news reach her, and changing the topic when she asked questions to understand sad things in life. And many such things.

It does not mean you shouldn't do such things for a girl or a woman; you help when necessary and let her do things mostly for herself. One cannot gain valuable experience otherwise. You may make some mistakes in differentiating when to help and when to let her do her things, but you will get better at it.

Instead, we all did everything for her. After refusing all our gestures initially, she accepted it as her way of life. She believed she would always be caught when she fell."

I was frozen. I walked for a week, feeling deeply sad about Angela, and then for all the girls and boys out in the world. While growing up, I decided I would never go to college. I simply wanted to work on wood and build new things. After hearing my grandma, I decided to help as many people as possible, went to college, and studied psychology.

I worked with Fun Bob, and fortunately, I was able to help him get over his guilt that he believed he was the one responsible for Angela's death that day. Now Bob has a lovely family and works as a builder in Boston.

I build creative furniture and work in the interiors of buildings for my living. And I put to use my studies in psychology and world experience to counsel as many people as possible."

Kamali is fully absorbed in Pat's story.

"I am so sorry, Uncle Pat. I will pray for my Aunt Angela's peace. I now understand why my father explains almost everything to me. My parents ask me to take care of simple things myself, such as making my schedule and cleaning my plates. I also designed some stuff using my father's computer."

"Very good. I have shared this story with your father, Kamali, years ago. Next time, I will share a different story. I know today you will feel sad having heard the story of Angela and me. But it's important. Sadness preserves happiness and happy memories."

Kamali nods yes, thoughtfully.

"Thank you, Uncle Pat. I will see you next week."

"Okay, dear! Bye for now."

Kamali comes running to her parents. Naren and Uma are discussing something, sitting on the couch. Kamali hugs her mom tight and says, "Thank you, Mom." And she jumps to Naren and does the same. Naren and Uma look at each other, with a question in their eyebrows and with lots of joy.

"Sweety! It seems you had a good call with Pat."

Kamali is still occupied with the depth of Angela's story, the sadness, and the lessons she learned. "Yes, Mom! A sad story, but necessary."

Kamali walks quietly to her study. Naren smiles kindly and holds Uma's hands.

What happens if we can't feel sad?

4

Dad! Why do you always question?

When most of the countries in the world are celebrating summer, Australia is experiencing its winter. Surya is walking with his son Krishtopher along the beach.

Surya experienced his first 'Summer Christmas,' almost two decades ago, thanks to Rachel. Surya and Naren are friends since their school years. Naren loves to meet people and has an active social life. One day he almost dragged Surya to a reunion with friends where Rachel and Surya met. It was love at the first meeting, if not at first sight. After graduation, Surya found a job and joined Rachel, who wanted to move back to Australia.

"Dad! How was your day?"

"What is a 'day,' Krishtopher?"

Ah, oh! Krishtopher knows what he is faced with now. Surya is in his mode of inquiry. He will not stop asking questions. They are odd questions, according to Krishtopher. Krishtopher confirmed with most of his classmates that none of their parents ask as many odd questions as his father.

Krishtopher is the name given by his parents, Rachel, who loves the Indian avatar Krishna, and Surya, who respects Rachel's dad, Christopher, for his character. Christopher was a soulful man who built his business empire through honest work and unwavering commitment.

Surya is a professor of philosophy and a writer. When he was in college, he studied under an Indian teacher and Guru, Vethathiri Maharishi, who lived a contemplative life.

From that time, Surya treats understanding the impact of his decisions on different people and things as the first priority before he acts. He thoroughly studies cause and effect in all facets of life.

Throughout his career, Surya has studied many authors and evolved people. With his commitment to helping his friends and family be better thinkers, Surya has made it a practice that he does not leave any conversation without posing at least one question.

After all, for thousands of years, India, Surya's country of origin, was known as the land of inquiry and practice. After repeated invasions by foreign forces that damaged the culture, including the British rule, India lost her edge. Not all her people practice Yoga and inquiry nowadays. Fortunately, some daring souls question the status quo and move the country forward in many fields.

Surya believes if people understand the consequences of their thoughts and actions, not only as an idea but with all their heart and feelings, they can shape their lives the way they want. As a committed and practical philosopher, he always looks for 'what causes what – cause and effect,' and 'how is one thing different from the other? – discrimination.'

Sometimes it makes conversing with him tiring for his friends and family. But his friends adapt, and he also adapts with them to go easy and not always ask question after question.

"Dad! I just asked a simple question that any person asks another. 'Hey! How was your day?' The person asked would answer, 'It was great, or it was not so great.' Simple questions and simple responses. Why are you asking what a day is?"

Surya smiles and looks at his son, affectionately, "There is a reason I'm asking this question, Krishtopher."

"Well, the day is the time between sunrise and sunset."

"You asked an interesting question - How is your day? There is time. And there is what we do during that time. What are you actually asking me when you ask me how my day was? During this time, I did many things. I talked and worked with many people. Are you asking how the day was or how I dealt with things and people in my day?"

"Is there any difference, Pa?"

"I think so, Krishtopher. Could you look at your experience and tell me if there is a difference?"

Krishtopher ponders for a while. "Yes. There is."

"What is it?"

"I feel happy when I get what I want. I feel upset when I don't get what I want. And when I feel happy or upset, I just feel the time spent as either good or bad. I don't want a bad time and only want a good time."

"Okay, great. When do you notice the difference between time and how you use it?"

"When I don't expect anything."

"How?"

"I don't know. I just feel playful when I'm not expecting something from you or mom. There are changes from the way the sun is in the morning, afternoon, and evening. The air feels different, and so do many little things around me. I notice the changes and also observe what I do. I don't even think to observe. I'm just aware."

True, Surya remembers how his son plays with the gadgets, sits in the swing, seemingly does nothing, and keeps walking a lot. When Krish does an activity with complete absorption, it is a sight to behold.

Anyways, Krishtopher hardly asks for things except maybe his favorite food on occasion, or for an extended time when all his family watches Star Trek. During those times he is inflexible and more easily gets upset.

Surya admires Kristopher's honesty and thinks that the world's problems can easily be solved if adults were as honest as kids. He sincerely wishes that Krishtopher will always maintain his simplicity and truthfulness with himself, if not with anyone else.

More than ever, Surya is intense in questioning as he is working on a presentation on the mind. In his childhood, Surya considered the mind only as a collection of thoughts. Even then, he was aware that the mind is not an organ such as the brain. He thought of it as an invisible field in one's body that can't be located.

He studied various books by great people from India during his research. He put together his understanding of the mind as a field that functions through the interaction of its components. The components he listed are, 'Thinking, Feelings, Emotions, Consciousness, Intellect, and the Sense of I, which is also called the Ego.'

For Surya, language is both emotional and logical. When both the logic and emotions work in tandem, there is great clarity and beauty to his writing. Language and Philosophy are his favorite subjects since childhood.

Surya thinks further. *"It is becoming fashionable to say, 'I created a great day,' 'I chose my thoughts,' and 'I chose my emotions.' Such words and phrases are usually uttered by people who follow an author or a Guru, who say that we choose what we do in every moment.*

Those authors and Gurus who are genuine, recognize choice. But what about people who proclaim that they are the followers of the person or the system? Maybe some do, but generally, no one proclaims that they're followers of a toothpaste brand they use. In most cases, I find that the moment one feels a need to proclaim that they follow something, and they are angrily defending their choice, they likely have lost objectivity and reduced their capacity to discriminate.

How many people who say such things are really aware that they are making each choice? Do they really create their day? Why is there so much difference between theory and practice? Why is there so much difference between what one can do and what one says one can do?

Don't we feel, especially when things don't go the way we want, that it is a bad day or a sad day? When things go the way we want, we say it is a great day. What is the disadvantage of being truthful, to say, "that is how I experience my day," plainly, without covering up?

Why do we like to believe we should be something? And subsequently lose touch with who and where we are?"

Krishtopher is playing on the beach as Surya is walking along with his thoughts.

***

"Forces beyond your control can take away everything you possess except one thing, your freedom to choose how you will respond to the situation." – Viktor Frankl.

Rachel writes this quote from Viktor Frankl in her journal. She had a day of tedious labor. The software she is building has not yet yielded the correct results.

She was born and raised in Australia in a 'world' neighborhood. Her parents were keen on self-development and about mingling with different cultures. Hence, they found a community in an apartment complex where people from different cultures live together. Most of them happened to be working in embassies of different countries.

When Rachel was young, she spent a lot of time with Hannah from Austria. Hannah's mom would always tell them a quote or two from Viktor Frankl's "Man's search for Meaning". Frankl's approach to life and his tale of surviving the holocaust fascinated young Rachel. She bought a copy of the book and had it autographed by Hannah and her mom. She still feels as if Viktor Frankl had signed her book through them.

Rachel is a seasoned and accomplished programmer and software developer. When Rachel finishes her work, she usually joins Surya and Krishtopher in their walk, always writing a few words in her journal before joining them.

Rachel is a sincere practitioner of any theory she finds appealing. She loves the Viktor Frankl book and has been practicing following a quote from it in her day to day life. She reviews her day in the evening and finds a quote that appeals to her day's challenges.

"This one is tough to adopt in life, but I want to," Rachel says to herself. She closes her journal and walks up to the beach. She thinks about the quote and the practical application of it in her daily life.

"When someone at work is angry and they shout at you, how can you pause and choose at least a neutral response, if not a kind one? It does not even require anyone to shout. Just a quick expression of irritation or a look is enough to unsettle my feelings. And then it's all downhill. I don't recognize I have a choice to respond. My feelings lead me, and I follow."

One of Rachel's greatest strengths is her ability to take failures sportively. Another is her tireless perseverance to practice what she knows in day to day life.

"Hi, ma!" Krish comes running towards her. Surya walks towards Rachel and holds her hands gently.

"Did the demo work?"

"Unfortunately no, but I won't say it's a bad day or a sad day!"

Surya chuckles. "Oh, I see! How come?"

"I will tell you later."

The three of them enjoy the breeze and walk for thirty minutes before it is time for dinner.

"I spoke to Naren yesterday!" Surya does not contain his excitement.

"He is a keen student of life. He takes advice or a suggestion to heart and applies it."

Rachel enjoys hearing about Naren. She loves how Surya reaches out to people and strengthens the bond with his friends. Naren is the same way. And Surya appreciates Rachel supporting him as well as being the finance minister of the home.

Her sharp mind which takes care of the household and the family's financial plans also serves as Surya's compass and anchor. Rachel behaves as a true scientist, honestly testing the philosophies by practicing them in life.

"Ma! Why won't you say it is a bad day?"

"Krish! That is because…" Rachel opens her journal and reads out aloud.

"*Forces beyond your control can take away everything you possess except one thing, your freedom to choose how you will respond to the situation. – Viktor Frankl.*"

"And I am going to practice this."

"It is all about pausing and finding the truth." Krish chuckles and goes on singing a song she likes.

"And about meaningful existence," Surya tells himself and opens up his computer.

Surya has been sharing with his friends the need to pause and how pausing is like using the brake when you drive your car. Just as the car and the people inside are saved by the timely use of the brake, the human experience is harmonious when you defer a difficult reaction such as anger.

"How is the paper coming along?" Rachel asks.

"I'm writing a summary. Tell me what you think!"

"The day is neither sad nor happy. I make it so. And I can only recognize it to be so if I apply conscious effort to pause my flow of emotions in one direction and redirect them. My mind, which is a field of interaction of intellect, consciousness, the sense of I or Ego, emotions, thinking and feeling, can bring itself to order by deciding to be in charge."

"Dad! Then who is the I, and is it different from your mind? What is the difference between 'I' and 'the sense of I'?"

Krish asks and then reverts to his singing.

"Surya! Your paper is not done!" Rachel laughs.

"Thankfully, so!" Surya bows to Krish, who keeps giggling.

Surya tosses around in bed that night, thinking of Krish's question. He does not want to recall the answer, the difference between 'the mind and I - the self,' from what he read. He wants to feel the answer, experience it himself, and explain it in simple terms in his paper.

The ceiling fan sends a cool breeze to his face. Though it is cold weather, Surya keeps the fan on for some time for Krish. Krish watches the lines of the blades of the fan disappear from his eyes quickly and falls asleep. Surya does not turn off the fan yet. Rachel pulls another blanket and reminds Surya to stop the fan. Surya obliges and then walks to the living room. He lays on the couch, switches on the fan in the living room, and watches the blades quickly disappear.

In about half an hour, he jumps off the couch and rushes to the bedroom to grab his journal. Rachel wakes up from his movement but falls back to sleep instantly.

Surya writes enthusiastically in his journal.

"You can't see electricity with your naked eye. You may see a crowd of electrons in a wire with a special instrument, but never their flow, which is electricity.

Obviously, you can see what electricity does. What it moves – for example, a fan, a car, a bulb it lights up, etc. The same can be said about 'the I which is the real self.'

Science can describe how food is digested, how breathing occurs, how vision within the eye happens, etc. But it can never tell what causes all the movements.

It cannot measure the life within us. Life - the force within us - perhaps is the "real I." Maybe one of the types of flow of life within our bodies is the mind. You cannot directly measure or know the force, which is 'self or I.' But we can experience its capabilities by studying our thoughts, feelings, emotions, and actions."

Surya begins to understand what Vethathiri Maharishi once said to him. Surya asked him what it means that Vethathiri Maharishi said the mind is the extension of life force. The Guru answered, "Smoke is an extension of fire. Similarly, the mind is an extension of the life force."

Surya thinks further. *When he throws a stone in a still pond, he sees ripples. Aren't the ripples and the still-water of the same water? Similarly, aren't the waves and the water at the bottom of the sea the same water?*

The difference between them is movement. And the parts of the mind are very mobile. Sometimes thoughts rush, and other times are lazy. Feelings change and move. Emotions exhibit the same tendency. Intellect also needs to shift its attention from one thing to another to study and differentiate things.

He continues to write in his journal. "We make the 'Sense of I - Ego' into an impediment when we make it fixed on images we like. Isn't it? Then it has a life of its own, determining our choices and controlling our lives.

This sense is merely a shadow of the real, the life force. I create this sense of I based on the body - how I look, based on what I do, how I perform with respect to others, etc."

Surya writes more questions for himself before he falls asleep on the couch.

How does all this knowledge, my paper about the mind,
help a person in a practical way? Does it really have the
potential to make a person's life easier and better?

For example: How can it help a person or the people who
are counselors aid with suicide prevention?

How can I create interest in a common person to learn
about my work?

5

Naren's Vegetarian Dilemma

Kamali is getting ready for her classes. It is Naren's turn to cook today, and he just finished making the 'dosas' - rice crepes, the way Kamali likes; thin and crispy. Naren enjoys cooking, and he considers it similar to his meditation.

As usual, Naren, Kamali, and Uma sit on the floor to eat. Naren serves them the dosas with groundnut chutney.

Uma tells Naren that the chutney tastes good, but he could add a hint of salt for a better taste the next time. Naren thanks her.

"Kamali! How do you like your singing lessons?" Uma asks.

"I like it, ma. I need more practice." Kamali answers while closely examining the dosa on her plate.

"Anything wrong, dear?" Naren asks attentively.

"No, I'm just looking at how the same dosa has different textures and shades of color in different parts of its body."

Naren looks affectionately at Kamali. Kamali sometimes treats her dolls so tenderly and affectionately it's as if they are real babies. She does not scrub them much while cleaning because she thinks their tender bodies might get hurt. When Naren referred to cleaning her dolls, she corrected him that the dolls bathe just like humans. She bathes them with her body wash and treats them just as she treats her own body.

It does not surprise Naren that Kamali used 'body' when describing a part of the dosa.

"Okay, honey. The next time Father is making dosas, you can stand with him, watch how the color changes and the texture becomes different. Would you eat now while it is hot?" asks Uma.

"Alright, alright, ma." Kamali quietly eats.

All three chew their food very well now. Naren keeps it to 24 times while Uma and Kamali do not count but still chew well.

As he eats, Naren silently thanks the video makers, the YouTube platform, and the presenter R. Madhavan who spoke about the importance of chewing food well. Counting helps him to complete the task entirely.

Naren thinks. "It is incredible to have an assembly of useful information on the internet. One needs to use their discernment to differentiate useful information. Yet, the availability gives a person multiple options and the opportunity to learn to find the good amongst the crowd."

Naren considers the digital technological revolution as similar to the industrial revolution that completely transformed how societies evolved.

Kamali finishes eating, washes her plate, and walks into her study for her classes.

Uma speaks to Naren. "Kamali is very sensitive. I'm not sure how she will manage when she mingles with kids who eat meat for almost every meal when we go to the United States."

"We didn't know either. We survived. We learned to adjust with other kids and made friends. Similarly, she will learn. We can't make her ready for everything. She will find her way," says Naren.

Naren had eaten meat in a few instances. He was ten years of age the first time he ate meat. He remembered how he couldn't resist the attraction to the smell of the meat getting cooked with all the spices. He was in a relative's home, and he ate merrily despite his decision to not eat meat.

That episode was four years after his decision at age six to not eat meat.

Since childhood, Naren has been very fond of baby goats. His decision to not eat meat, not even the first time for trying out, was when he watched a baby goat getting butchered in front of him. After that incident, Naren even asked his parents to bring home a baby goat to have as a pet.

Yet, when the goat was not in vision, and it was just a heap of meat that he did not see getting cooked in the pressure cooker, he did not say no.

In fact, he wanted to be invited to eat. Somehow, he lost the connection he made when he was six years old.

Since then, he's eaten meat at different stages in his life. When he finally made a commitment every time to *feel* the connection between the flesh inside the pressure cooker and its previous aliveness as a goat or chicken, he pledged to never eat meat again.

But Naren does not actively advocate for a vegetarian diet with everyone else or preach to everyone to become vegetarian whenever he sees an opportunity. He decided that it would be the same case with his daughter also. Kamali would need to decide for herself why or why not she would eat meat, and Uma and Naren do not cook meat at home.

Uma says, "Kamali's best friend Shreya likes to eat meat very much and also speaks about it a lot. Kamali asked me some questions after her last call with Shreya."

Shreya is a lovely child, a kindred spirit to Kamali. She lives in Somerset, New Jersey, and is a daughter of Sam and Rupali. Sam's full name is Samaveda Ram Prasad.

Sam is a vegetarian, and Rupali allows herself to eat eggs sometimes, but not meat. But when Shreya wanted to eat meat, they did not stop her. They take Shreya two or three times a week to eat out.

"What kind of questions?" Naren asks Uma.

"How will you get your protein if you don't eat eggs or meat? How will you be able to compete with others in sports that you love? Questions like that. And Kamali is worried if she might lag behind the others."

A child's biggest worry is not to lag behind the others, thinks Naren. He knows this worry as he struggled with it for many years, extending into his adult life.

"Okay! Let us see what we can do. Next time, please include me in your conversation with Kamali. We'll discuss it as a family and work on clarifying the myths and facts."

Uma and Naren begin their work for the day. Uma is continuing the program she is building, and Naren is writing a speech.

Alongside, he is thinking hard on the questions that resurfaced for him.

1. Why shouldn't he be the advocate for not killing animals?

2. What about all destructive practices in the world that create comfort and evolution for humans? Such as unnecessary travel by flying and driving that pollutes the air and the unexamined production of things that create so much waste. Should he boycott them all and advocate for everyone also to do so?

3. How would he go about life? What job would he accept? Which people would he relate with? Will he stop connecting with people who support the destruction in practices that he disagrees with?

4. If he believes it's not his place to judge, then is he running away from the responsibility for his way of life and what he thinks is right?

Naren stops as his head hurts from his continuous thoughts and the emotions that jostle his mind.

After a peaceful lunch, he picks up a book written by the legendary Swami Vivekananda.

Swami Vivekananda was a brave saint who treaded unchartered and unfriendly waters and dealt with the calmest as well as the most brutal of the population in his time. His impact in the United States was so much that a street was named after him in Chicago.

When Swami Vivekananda visited the States in 1893, he made a heart touching and majestic speech where he addressed the gathering as, 'Dear sisters and brothers of America.' What happened after the address was magical. People were drawn to him, and many followed him wherever he went.

Naren read Vivekananda's commentary on Patanjali Yoga Sutras for an hour. He finds a certain clarity within himself and goes about his work.

Meanwhile, Kamali is on the swing and is deeply lost in her book. At the rate she reads, Naren needs to borrow a book every day in the library.

"She is just like how I was," smiles Naren as he keeps making calendar appointments on his computer for the upcoming weeks.

Precisely at 5 pm, Uma receives a call. It is Rupali from New Jersey. Uma looks happy and also a bit worried while she hands the phone to Kamali. Kamali disappears into the study.

Anyone who makes the first contact with Kamali might prematurely conclude that Kamali is more of an introvert than an extrovert. Uma and Naren do not believe in stereotypes, especially after experiencing how flexible their daughter is and how she adapts well to different conditions.

Naren believes that there are no introverts or extroverts per se. There are only tendencies practiced for a long time, and they can be reversed with effort, focus, and guidance. Kamali fluently converses after she breaks the ice with a stranger, and these days, she initiates conversations more often than not.

About two hours pass. Kamali comes out from the study with lots of excitement.

"Mom! I learned something new today. Shreya taught me a new way to multiply numbers, which is way faster than I've done."

"Good, dear."

"I also taught her some Tamil words at her request. I am surprised that she wants to learn Tamil. She already speaks English and Spanish fluently. So, we have a plan for each teaching each other for the next few weeks."

"Oh, Good! I am glad."

"Dad! I have a question for you. Shreya says eating meat is necessary, but I don't feel it's necessary. I am healthy, and you and mom look healthy. I have not seen any animal being killed in front of me as you have experienced. Still, I feel sad; so many animals are being killed for their flesh. Is that right? Isn't it wrong?"

"Many animals are killed for leather also."

"Dad, I don't think killing animals for food is a good thing, is it? When there are so many other things to eat, isn't killing and eating animal flesh wrong? I said it is so to Shreya."

"And..."

"She looked sad and confused and said she would talk to her mom. I didn't know what else to say. Then I asked her about her techniques in math and changed the conversation."

"I see. You know, Kamali, sometimes staying sad and confused is not bad. When I face a dilemma, I'm sad and confused too."

"Dad! I didn't know what to do next when she looked that way."

"I understand."

"What do you think? Isn't killing animals for food wrong and bad?"

"Kamali! I can tell you what it is for me. I'm not able to tolerate the pain and the loss of opportunity for an animal to live its natural life. From that basis and for me, it is wrong."

"Dad! If only some people like you and I think that way, and all the rest think it's okay, animals will keep getting killed. How can we stop it?

When we went to the village to see grandma and grandpa, I saw this open butcher shop. There was this huge man with a big belly, and he was dragging a goat inside. I was terrified and sad. After some time, the man came out and washed his hands. I knew what he did. He was so heartless."

Naren is surprised to hear this; his attempts to take Kamali on a different route to their home seems to have failed. Kamali might have gone to the department store at the corner of their street, where she could have easily noticed what happened at the butcher shop.

"Do you consider Shreya as heartless?"

"No! She does not kill animals."

"But she eats them."

Kamali looks sad and confused.

"Honey! I think we have two things going on. The first is the subject of killing animals for food. And the second is how we relate with each other when we think what another person does is wrong. Do we get angry at them? Do we hate them? Or do we feel scared of them? And it's all the more confusing when they're our friends, right?"

Kamali thinks for a while. "Uh-huh."

"You know, Kamali, I've been thinking about this subject for a long time. And I want to share with you a story that helped me get to some clarity. Would you like to hear it?"

"Yes, Dad," Kamali answers immediately.

"This is a story told by Swami Vivekananda. He learned about the story from Bhagavad Gita, in which Lord Krishna transmitted himself to the great warrior Arjuna, at the battlefield.

On the battlefield, Arjuna hesitates to proceed with the war-plan and feels dejected. Until that time, Arjuna felt justified that the war was right, and for the right cause.

Almost all people who know the story would agree that Arjuna's side had a just cause. And yet, he feels dejected as he sees his kith and kin, relatives who he grew up with, and his teachers, against him. With this backdrop in mind, I will tell you the story.

A young boy who wanted to be a saint went to a forest. He found a secluded place where he meditated and practiced Yoga for a long time. Several years went by. One day when he was sitting under a tree, dry leaves fell on his head. He looked up and noticed a crow and crane fighting.

He felt anger and glanced at them, uttering, "How dare you throw leaves on my head!"

His yogic power was intense such that at his glance, the birds fell and died. Perhaps they had burnt to ashes, also.

The boy felt overjoyed at the development of his power. After a while, he went to the nearby village to beg for his food, a usual routine.

He went to a home, stood at the footsteps of the entrance, and said, "Mother! Give me food."

In ancient India, it is considered a privilege to feed such dedicated practitioners of Yoga and sainthood. He heard a female voice, "Wait for a moment, my son."

A few minutes went by.

The boy got angry and thought, "You lowly woman, how dare you make me wait! You have no idea of my powers!"

Immediately he heard the same voice again, "Son! Don't think too much of yourself. I am neither a crow nor a crane."

The boy was shocked. He fell at the woman's feet when she came out to offer him food and said, "Mother! How did you know my thoughts? Are you a yogi? How long have you been practicing? Would you teach me your methods?"

"Son, I am no Yogi. I am a common woman. All I know is to do my duty well. When I asked you to wait, I was attending to my husband, who is ill. Until I got married, I focused on taking care of my aged parents as my main duty. Now, I apply the same care to my husband and immediate family. My Yoga is my duty.

As I was doing my duty with cheerfulness, I was illumined and could sense things. I read your thoughts and what you had done in the forest. If you want to know more than I know, then you may go to the market in the next town where you will find a particular Vyaadha. People call him Dharma Vyaadha. He can teach you something that might give you more knowledge than you currently possess. Anyone in the town could bring you to him if you tell them who you are looking for."

Vyaadha, at that time in India, was the lowest class of people, mostly hunters and butchers.

The boy thought, "A Vyaadha? Why should I go and meet a Vyaadha?"

But he was already humbled by a simple woman. And hence his mind was a little more open.

He reached the town and asked for Dharma Vyaadha. A man led him to Dharma Vyaadha's butcher shop. Dharma Vyaadha, a big man, was cutting meat with his large knives. The boy was in shock.

"Oh, God! Is this the man who will give me greater knowledge and help me get to a higher state in Yoga? He looks like a heartless demon."

Dharma Vyaadha looked up and said, "O Young Swami! Did the lady send you here? Kindly take a seat until I finish my business."

The young Yogi was rendered speechless again. He waited for the Vyaadha to finish his business.

After closing the shop, Dharma Vyaadha said to the Yogi, "Come, respected Swami! Let's go to my home."

They went to Vyaadha's home. Dharma Vyaadha gave the Yogi a seat, asked him to wait, and went inside his home.

He then washed his old father and mother, performed all the duties he could, such as massaging their feet, dressing them in fresh clothes, and asking what else they needed. When they said what they needed, he immediately tended to it to the best of his abilities.

After all his tasks were completed, he came to the Yogi and said, "Dear Swami! You have traveled a long way from home to see me. What can I do for you?

The young Yogi was observing how the Vyaadha was with his parents. The Yogi asked Dharma Vyaadha a few questions about the soul and God.

The Vyaadha gave a talk which forms a part of the great epic Mahabharata, called the Vyaadha-Gita. It is regarded as one of the highest accomplishments in Vedanta, a spiritual body of knowledge.

When Dharma Vyaadha finished his teaching, the young Yogi asked in astonishment, "Revered Sir! Why are you in this body of a Vyaadha and are doing such filthy, ugly, and cruel work? You have such knowledge that is not even found with saints who meditate for decades. Why do you need to do this lowest of the lower jobs?"

Dharma Vyaadha looked at the Yogi affectionately, "My son, no duty is ugly, no duty is impure. My birth placed me where I am and what I am doing. When I was a boy, I learned the trade. I make sincere attempts to do my duty well, in my job and in caring for my father and mother. I neither know any Yoga nor have aspired to be a saint. In my dedication to duty, I became unattached to what I do. Everything you have heard as answers to your questions has come from me being in this state."

Naren finishes the story and keeps talking to Kamali. "This story perplexed me so much. I heard it when I was young, and I wondered whether a murderer could justify his position, saying he is doing the duty with dedication, in the same lines. Then what is good and what is bad? However, what I deeply learned from the story is how I view the other person and myself.

The greatest of the saints did not find a place in Lord Krishna's work, but the Vyaadha did. If I judge a person by what they do alone, and without better knowledge of who they are, I will misunderstand the world and myself.

"Okay..." Kamali is thoughtful.

"Honey! I don't know about the butcher you saw and his character, kind or cruel. He could be either. To understand a person deeply, we need more information. Their appearance or what they do is not enough. We know somewhat of Shreya's character. Shreya will come to her conclusion about eating meat. And whatever she decides, I trust she will still remain your best friend."

"Yes, Dad."

"You could say the whole world is run by western inventions. Perhaps 90% of those great people, the inventors, are meat-eaters. Should we reject everything they did because that's true?"

"Hmm..." Kamali thinks more. Naren looks at her attentively. About fifteen minutes pass by. Kamali is tearful. Naren lets her be.

Kamali speaks with great effort. "Dad, I understand everything you said. So many animals are killed every day. It feels painful."

Naren hugs her and speaks. "I understand, my dear. Come to think of it, many things we do harm the lives of other species and the poor people. Do you remember we talked about plastics the other day? And you were telling how the birds would not collide with the planes because of less air traffic."

Kamali sobbingly says yes.

Naren looks at her affectionately. He lets her cry without interrupting her state of consciousness. After a while, he continues.

"Similarly, as each of us evaluates, we would change what we do. Maybe in some cases of necessity, we would still eat meat, knowingly and feeling sad about the loss of life of animals. And even in those cases, perhaps we will feel sad and also be thankful for the animals instead of making how the meat tastes on our tongues the only consideration."

Uma has been watching Kamali and Naren all this while. She walks to them and sits next to them. They all sit quietly, feeling joyful for being together and also feeling sad for all living beings that feel pain due to our decisions.

What happens if we don't feel pain at the plight of others?

6

Keep it simple, Papito!

Antonio keeps on drawing. It has been four hours since he started. There is a beautiful photograph on a stand to his left. He is doing a pencil sketch, which is just beginning to look like the photograph. He keeps a lid on all his excitement to maintain a 100% focus on his strokes. Each stroke caresses the paper with incredible precision. He has not eaten since he woke up. When his wife Natalia entered his drawing-room, she sensed his unwavering focus, bubbling anger, and quietly kept the sandwich plate on a table and left.

She pleaded with him to have a mini dining table in his vast drawing-room. After quite some resistance, Antonio agreed. The drawing-room, also his study, is his only temple and his artwork his only religion. As usual, the sandwich is waiting for him on the lonely table in the corner of the room.

Antonio is a lovely man in his fifties. He has a child-like cherubic face. He is often the life of the party he joins. His kids and wife love him very much. He gave up smoking and drinking alcohol in one stroke for his love for them. He wants to live long, and he badly wants to beat all the men in his family ancestry. His goal is to achieve at least 75 years of life in good health.

In fourth grade, Antonio made a brilliant pencil sketch. His parents could not believe it to be the work of a fourth grader. But they only celebrated it as they watched him do it.

Antonio's teacher, who did not witness the young genius's work as he did it, called him a liar for not admitting that the sketch was made, he assumed, by an adult. Antonio was deeply hurt. He returned home, put his pencil down, and hadn't raised it again until six months ago, forty-nine years after his art teacher's incorrect and harsh judgment.

Antonio never carried any ill-will for his teacher, but he shut himself down, believing no one would support his creativity. Not understanding why, after his youngest daughter's birth seven months ago, his interest in drawing resurfaced. He wanted to make a sketch of her, and after completing it did not stop at that single desire.

Antonio is a soft-spoken man who has never yelled at his loved ones, but he expresses his displeasure in measured words coated with subdued anger when his art is interrupted. Natalia, a sensitive and sensible woman, feels Antonio's hidden anger and does not engage it. She leaves him undisturbed unless he misses two meals in a row. After then, Antonio will have to do everything to get Natalia to speak to him. One time, she did not speak for two full days. Natalia did not walk around angry. She quietly did all the household jobs and observed a 'fast of words - silence,' with everyone. Antonio knew how painful she felt inside and immediately corrected himself thereafter.

Antonio's skill improves each day. The pencil sketch looks just like the photograph. He looks at his watch and notes that in another hour, lunch will be served. Antonio sets up five alarms with a space of three minutes between them leading to lunch. He chose the loudest alarm-tone, so he will hear the reminder no matter how lost he is in his work. When it's ten minutes to lunch time, he diligently picks up the plate and eats the delightful sandwich. He thinks Natalia's preparations are time-proof, that it tastes delicious even when eaten hours after. He wears a proud smile on his lips and walks to the kitchen with the empty plate. "I ate it."

Natalia chuckles and asks, "When?"

"Hey! Hey! That you should not ask, I have not missed a meal, let alone two since your 'Satyagraha.' Did I say the word correctly?"

"You did. For tomorrow, I'd like you to have a smoothie at 11 a.m., but only if you have not had breakfast until that time."

Natalia has a way around people, and her kids are her best trainers in developing such capacity. Forty-year-old Natalia married fifty-three-year-old Antonio two years ago. They both have incredible warmth, love, and interest in life.

Antonio welcomed Natalia's fourteen-year-old daughter, Alexa, as a godsend in his life. Alexa takes care of Solange, the youngest, just as her lovely mom does. Natalia, also a businesswoman, manages her family restaurant in a distant town with her loyal team's assistance. It's at the restaurant where Antonio and Natalia first met.

Natalia has a profound interest in cultures and studying women and men of great character. When she read about the principles of Satyagraha from Mahatma Gandhi's autobiography, 'My Experiments with Truth,' she felt deeply moved. She has experienced two schools of thought; one that is supportive of Gandhi's methods and another against, shared by her friends from India. She is open to hearing all points of view and does not engage in arguments. Her understanding of Satyagraha is what she implements in her daily life with her family.

'Satya,' the Sanskrit word which means 'truth,'' and agraha means 'insistence.' It could be translated to mean "insistence on truth" or "holding onto truth."

There is some truth to what happens when Antonio skips meals regularly and exhausts his energy. Her non-cooperation movement with him, Satyagraha, is often done with a 'speech fast,' without which neither Antonio nor anyone in her family can manage. She understands the shortcoming that her family might not look deeply into the impact of their actions because of their desire and subsequent efforts to get her to speak again. So, she artfully points them to look at their actions which she protests.

Antonio has a sweet tooth. All his life, he did many different things, but he struggles to avoid sweets and bread. He is overweight. Genetically he has a disposition to quickly add weight, and he feels discouraged that his efforts do not yield results. When he feels discouraged, he eats sweets and bread, more than what he usually does.

Antonio often exercises with Victor Valdes. They are good friends and workout partners, and they both follow a custom fitness program made by their trainers. While Antonio is happy for his friend, he is disappointed that he does not get the same results. So, he gives up exercising for a while, and when he resumes again, he has an uphill climb. He overdoes his exercises to make up, but it doesn't help and causes injuries.

Thus, this cycle continues.

All the family is at lunch, and it's a joyous moment. Margarita, their housemaid, cooks excellent meals. They all share jokes, pass around food, feed each other just as mothers do with their babies, and have a great time.

"I'm going to make sure I never miss a meal with family," Antonio Roberto thinks. After lunch, he returns to his study and immerses himself in finishing the sketch. He feels satisfied with his restraint on the meal. He did not drink any soda and didn't overeat. Alexa enters the study and Antonio looks at her affectionately.

"Papito, could we go for a walk by the beach in the evening?" asks Alexa. Antonio Roberto thinks for a while and says, "Okay, Alexa."

He knows he will complete the sketch before the walk time, usually six o'clock in the evening. Whenever Alexa has this request, there is always something to talk about.

"What could the topic be?" thinks Antonio Roberto as he picks up his pencil. He sets three alarms with five minutes between them from five-forty pm. And in a few minutes, he becomes one with his sketch, pencils, and the studio.

At six o'clock, Alexa and Antonio are walking on the beach. Antonio is always punctual with Alexa. After a few meetings with Antonio, Alexa had already adopted him as her father in her heart, well ahead of the marriage. Alexa finds him reliable, sweet, and above all, a friend. She talks about her problems comfortably with him. Yet, Antonio feels there is more to do to earn 'the father' status properly.

"Tell me, Alexa. Is there something specific you want to talk to me about?"

"Hmm, yes, Papito. But I feel awkward and scared to talk about it."

"Okay. Is this something to do with any of the boys in your class?"

Alexa is surprised. "How did you know?"

"I don't know anything, honey, just a hunch. Besides, I was a boy noticing girls when I was your age. Did you tell Natalia about it?"

"Yes, yesterday. I also told mom I would talk to you today about it."

"Okay. Go ahead, honey!"

"There is this boy, Jorge. He keeps asking me to go with him for dinner. I don't like him. But I'm afraid of him."

"Would you like to go to dinner with any other boy?"

"Only as a friend, Papito, and with at least one more friend - boy or a girl, if it's dinner. If it's lunch, then I'm comfortable going with some other boy to the school canteen. It doesn't mean anything."

"Oh, it doesn't?"

"Yes. Dinner means somehow the friendship is becoming romantic. This is not the age for me."

"I understand. When a girl agrees to go with a boy, even lunch can be romantic for him! Why are you scared of Jorge, dearest?"

"He could hurt me if I reject him."

"Hmm, that's a reasonable worry indeed. Alexa, I will go with you tomorrow. Could you introduce Jorge to me?"

"What?" Alexa is shocked.

"I will not fight with the boy. How have you avoided him so far?"

"I always said I needed to be home for dinner."

"Okay." Antonio thinks for a while. They both walk silently. The beach is serene; the bluish water extends beyond what the eyes can see and is beautiful.

"Oh, shoot!" Antonio is about to fall, and Alexa holds him with all her strength. She can feel his pain, and she gently leads him to have a seat on the sand. She sits next to him.

"Papito! Did you run today?"

"Yes, dear."

"Why, Papito? The doctor asked you to wait for two more weeks, didn't he?"

Antonio is holding his left knee, which is shivering from the pain. With considerable effort, he begins to speak. Alexa asks him not to speak, walks to the shore, and soaks her shawl in the cool water. She gently removes Antonio's hands and uses the wet cloth like an ice pack. It's an inadequate substitute for the ice pack, but the gesture itself relaxes and touches Antonio's heart.

"Papito! Should I get some help to take you home?"

"No, dear. I will be alright in a while. Let's sit, enjoy the evening and talk for a bit."

Alexa repeats soaking her shawl in the cold water and pressing it against his knee.

After a few times, Antonio asks her to sit next to him and stops her from going to the water. He takes her hands and holds them dearly.

"Thank you, my child."

'Don't mention it, Papito. I'm curious; you could have waited according to the doctor's instructions. Why did you run today?"

Antonio sees her concern. She does not make any effort to hide it.

"What have I done for such an angel to enter my life!" Antonio is deeply grateful.

"I want to live long, my dear. All the men in my family, going back as far as I know, did not live beyond sixty-five. In fact, only one made it to sixty-five. Everyone died between fifty-five and sixty-five years old. I'm a happy man as I am now, but I want to see you and Solange grow up for as long as possible. I want to hold your mama's hands and walk on this beach, and await you, Solange, and your future husbands coming to visit us."

"That would be nice, Papito. You will definitely make it."

"I'm not so sure, honey." Antonio has not given up his fear. When he was a young boy, he lost his mother and then his father. And in a few years after marriage, he lost his first wife.

"How is running today, when the doctor has asked you to wait for two weeks, going to help you live a long life?"

"I felt okay to run. And I feel my years are numbered. So, I ran."

"Running is not like the sketch where you can spend many hours, Papito! Your knees can't take it."

"My dear! In every area of my life, I am catching up. I gave up drawing for some silly reason, and now I want to make up for all the time lost. Now that I know I can put so many hours in drawing, I want to fix other areas of my life."

"Papito! You have given us a great life already, as you are. Why are you torturing yourself so much?"

Antonio is speechless. The moonlight accentuates the subtle and profound pain that appears in his face.

He breaks into tears. "Not enough, dearest, not enough."

"Says who, Papito?" Alexa gently hugs her father.

"I want to earn your respect as your father, a role model that you can be proud of."

"But you already have, even before you and mom got married."

"What are you saying, Alexa?"

"There was no man who ever looked at me with such kindness as you did, Papito. You did so at our very first meeting. I knew I found my father instantly. That kindness you show me only increases every day. I can never repay it. You are my father and my dearest friend."

It feels a bit uncomfortable to cry in front of his lovely daughter. But the depth of her love pushes him through his discomfort and he cries. He buries his face in her lovely hands. Alexa sheds tears too.

"Keep it simple, Papito! One day at a time. If the doctor asks only to walk, then only do that. You know this too well. You asked me to keep it simple when I was struggling with my bale dance lessons. Then I trained one small move each day and mastered only that move."

"Yes, dear."

Antonio knows why he didn't keep it simple. *"When you let your emotions and imagination guide you, sometimes they take you too far away. You can use your mind to slow down and keep it simple."*

He feels Alexa's love in the way she is with him. It feels so much better when he hears what she thinks of and shares how she feels around him. It is great to love and be loved.

"Thank you, dear. Tomorrow we will see the boy. What's his name again?"

"Jorge, Papito."

"Okay. Jorge, nice to meet you, son." Antonio tells himself. Alexa and Antonio enjoy the quietness at the beach and the happy glow from the moonlight. Perhaps the moon is delighted at the experience of love, the unspoken force that can be felt from any distant corner of the universe.

When do you know it is time to stop what you do?

7

Useful theories

It's 7 a.m., and Rachel and Surya are preparing breakfast. They are quietly focused on their tasks. They love the freshness of the morning breeze. They always keep the windows of their beautiful home open for a few hours, even when the weather is cold.

Surya breaks the silence. He has been pondering several questions and is ready to share them with Rachel.

"How does all this knowledge, my paper about the mind, help a person in a practical way? Does it really have the potential to make a person's life easier and better?

For example: How can it help a person or the people who are counselors aid with suicide prevention?

How can I create interest in a common person to learn about my work?"

Rachel asks, "My dear! You intend to bring peace or balance to the reader's mind, yes? Have you thought about how it has helped you?"

She continues. "Doesn't the fact that you think and invest time to question things evolve your consciousness and conscience? Doesn't your contemplation pace your mind appropriately and keep it peaceful?"

Surya recognizes the truth in what Rachel says. His efforts to think have helped him. He knows that he is more patient with himself and others. He listens to others better than how he used to, and he's become a better counsel to his students.

"I am a philosophy professor. I'm also getting paid to think. What about a common man? The ice cream vendor pushing his cart in the sweltering heat of India. The girl at the cashier counter we spoke to yesterday in the supermarket.

If I simply give my paper to them or read it to them, will they find their way to evolve? What will they make of it? Why would they be motivated to read instead of worrying about their daily job?"

After asking Rachel his questions, he asks if he may join her friends' meet later in the evening. Rachel wasn't surprised. From time to time, Surya likes to ask one or more questions to Rachel and her friends. He does not give any counterarguments or opinions when they share their views on his work. He listens to them, makes notes, thanks them for their inputs, and continues his work. Surya wants all perspectives to be considered in his thinking process and is humble to accept that he does not know everything.

Rachel frequently meets with Uma, Kavya, Natalia, and Pat's life partner Deborah. They connect on Skype and exchange stories, life events, do online cooking sessions, or jam with their guitars.

They do not have a fixed schedule for their re-unions. One of them usually initiates a conversation with the others and arranges a meeting. They find it better than making a routine schedule each week or month.

Rachel texts her friends.

In a few minutes, she turns to Surya. "In a bit, Uma and Kavya will wake up in their morning and see the message. Everyone else is okay for you to join."

Surya acknowledges with a grateful thank you.

"Mom! Dad! I told you so many times to include me in making breakfast," Krish makes his entry to the kitchen.

"Sorry, Krishtopher! Mom did remind me, but I decided it might be better to let you rest after your late-night bedtime," says Surya.

"Okay," Krish says with a sigh.

"Surya! By the way, do you want to join us for our entire meeting?"

"No, honey! I don't want to take all of your time. I want to ask them the same questions I asked you about my research. I will leave the call after I hear everyone's responses."

The day passes quietly, with each of them engaging in their field of interest. Krish goes to his drawing room and continues the pencil sketch he has been making for two days, thanks to Antonio for his inspiration. Rachel is working on her computer and programming. Surya prepares for his class with a set of college students he began teaching last summer.

When one is living life joyfully or peacefully, time passes quickly in their experience. Such is the experience in Rachel and Surya's family and in the extended family of their close friends.

These friends and their families work diligently on their character to keep harmony in their hearts and homes. They were introduced to each other through school, work, and chance encounters at airports.

The values they share and interest in each other's welfare created immediate friendships that have become lifelong. The circle of friendship was started by Uma.

It is nine p.m. Rachel brews a pot of coffee and settles in for the meeting, along with Surya. Surya fine-tunes her guitar and sets up the call.

Everyone is connected, and they exchange lovely greetings to each other.

"So, what is brewing, Surya?"

"A question, Natalia," Surya answers.

"No wonder! Tell us," Deborah joins.

"I confess I need to share at least key parts of my write up on the human mind before I ask the question. It will take at most 5 minutes!"

"Go ahead, Surya! You have all our time," Uma smiles.

"Thank you." Surya shares the summary and puts forth the same questions.

"When I asked Rachel, she explained how I benefitted from the questions and the theories I have read and developed. I'm a professor, well paid, and have time to think and write. Let's take the case of someone who struggles in life to make both ends meet. How can I inspire such a person to read my work?"

"Well, why do you do this research anyway, Surya?" Kavya asks.

"Good question, Kavya! I have been intrigued by the different ways people approach life. For example, a person like me and a farmer who is toiling in their field for yields. They hope to produce a large volume of healthy crops, but they are unsure whether they will be successful due to many variable conditions. On the other hand, I get my salary without fail each month.

I have a calm life, while the farmer isn't calm, physically or emotionally. How would it occur for the farmer to sit and meditate? I want my work to bridge the gap between philosophy and practice for common people, and I have not been able to do so yet". Surya genuinely puts his question across. He continues.

"Of course, people who have a keen interest in philosophy and meditation will do no matter their circumstances. I am talking about the rest who don't have the inclination and whose eyes and heart are fixated on the day to day whether they are financially rich or poor. I trust unless I make my work relevant to their everyday life so it can help a person in their activities, there is not much use of me talking about my theories."

"There are so many Gurus in the world who have helped us understand what spirituality is, how the mind works, etc. Hasn't their work already made it relevant in the lives of people you describe, a laborer or a farmer, or even a white-collar person like us?" Deborah asks.

"Yes. At the same time, not all their messages reach the common person. In other words, a common person does not feel a need or motivation to learn about the mind. People like me could make things easier for those Gurus and experts by finding ways to create interest for the common folks. In fact, I want my work to just do that," Surya says.

"Why do you think what you write might be uninteresting or might not be understood by the common person?" Natalia asks.

Uma asks for permission and shares a view before Naren answers Natalia's question.

"See! Generally, a common man's mind is worried about something all the time. Until I was making a decent amount of money, I didn't think about anything else. Friends asked me to meditate, someone spoke to me about techniques to reach full potential, and another invited me to do their religious practices. I said a blind NO until I earned a good job and received a stable income for years. I think I can feel what Surya is getting at."

Surya says that is what he also considers as a common man's agenda. The agenda of securing a material life is so dominant to the common person that their mind has no space for anything else.

"If that's a common man's focus, why do they want to change it? Should they change it? A person will decide to study the mind and its potential when they want to," suggests Deborah.

Surya shares. "I do not intend to force a person to learn. I'm not even bothered about maximizing one's potential. *I want to bring a change such that a common person can learn to train their mind to not disrupt a peaceful state.*

In India, from recorded reports by the National Crime Records Bureau, 10,281 farmers committed suicide in 2019 and 10,159 students in 2018. Overall, about 139,000 people commit suicide in India every year, 10.5 per 100,000 of the population. If you look at Australia, 3046 deaths were reported in 2018, 12.2 per 100,000. The United States has 14.2 per 100,000. Overall, in the world, it is 11.6 per 100,000. Of course, these are recorded and reported numbers. The actuals could be higher.

And thoughtful researchers have often stated there are different causes for suicide, not just one reason. I agree, and I also firmly believe that the mind that wants to end life is not peaceful or balanced. I take the extreme case of ending life as one of the drivers for the cause I am campaigning, 'study and proper training of the mind.' I feel the need for many of us like me to come forward and contribute to a change in education; education about one's mind. What is the use of any other education without it?

All our educational systems focus on learning about tools and ways to make money and procure materials we need and want. Is that enough?

Additionally, unstructured and undisciplined work on improving oneself, offered by internet consultants and fake Gurus/experts, have further extended the problem. These fake personas promise people to improve their potential and charge hefty sums of money, extending the same approach we have adopted with materialistic goods. 'Buy my product, you will achieve great things, the mind's unlimited potential, and you will have everything you want.' And people fall for these personas, right?"

Everyone listens keenly and with genuine care. They feel the passion behind Surya's words.

"Please remind me. What is the synopsis of your work?" Deborah asks.

"It is said by many great Yogis. I did not invent any of this. I came up with metaphors to explain it to myself and to even a child. The self is like still water. Its movement, like a wave, is the mind, which includes thoughts, feelings, emotions, consciousness, intellect, and the sense of 'I.' *When we are self-aware, we can consciously control the mind and direct it to where we want.*

When we are forgetful of ourselves, not self-aware, and are lost in any aspect of the unaware mind, we are less able to deal with the world.

For example, I believe I can't help being angry whenever I see my boss. I eventually quit the job. Or I think 'I am a poor man,' and I reinforce that belief in my life by not seeking opportunities. Or I think, 'I am a rich man, I should remain so, but I am not sure if the wealth will last,' and with that confusion, I spoil my peace and work all the time."

Uma asks, "If a person does hard labor for their living and keeps thinking the same way all their life, how does that occur?"

"Because they don't think further?" Surya answers.

"Yes, a possibility is an imagination of the mind applied and tested. If the mind is a tool, could you use it more to do such things as imagination? It is a great example you mentioned when you said about still-water and waves. The source for both is water itself. I am not sure if anyone said this metaphor. But I quite like it. It offered me so much clarity," Uma says.

"Thank you. Someone might have said it also. I'm not aware. It's an easy comparison for me to understand the nature of our minds," Surya replies.

"Most people go to at least primary school. The education on what you said, Surya - self, mind, parts of the mind, and subsequent exercises to develop self-awareness - need to be taught experientially at the primary school level. I believe this is the only way for such knowledge to reach the majority of society. Teachers need to be trained to patiently and lovingly take this idea to the students," says Deborah.

"I agree fully," says Kavya.

"Yes, self-awareness brings flexibility in thinking and creativity in imagination. When we are coached to build a good work ethic early in our lives to supplement self-awareness, we can more easily put our attention on anything and stay focused," says Rachel.

"The truth is we have only finite opportunities in the job market or entrepreneurship. Even with all this knowledge, people will still end up doing blue-collar jobs," says Natalia.

"True. But we don't know what kind of future we will create if everyone is equipped with this knowledge. And secondly, even if we know that the future will have the same type of job markets as we have now, at least we will be peaceful and happy.

When we do not judge ourselves badly that we are not smart, when we no longer like or dislike any emotion as we know how to change it when we are self-aware, it is easy to be peaceful and happy," says Kavya.

"Say that again!" Deborah.

"See, when I am self-aware, I am driving the chariot with expert knowledge from experience, and the horses obey me. Here I compare the chariot with my body and the subtle aspects of mind, emotions, thoughts, consciousness, etc., with the horses. Such awareness maintains a constant state of peace and joy. When this awareness goes out the window, I forget who I am and experience happiness or peace or joy only when I get what I want. In life, we don't always get what we want. Besides, the happiness I arrive at by getting what I want is temporary," explains Kavya.

"Yup," agrees Deborah.

"Surya! I want to go back to a question you posed about how your work could help prevent suicide? Or could it? You said the mind has a role. I think when you believe you don't control anything and also when you think you can control everything, that is when you lose balance," says Natalia.

"Thanks, Natalia! Yes. I think all the work on the mind ultimately revealed two things. The first is to really see and own that I can choose my responses to everything. The second is to be humble that even if it's true that I choose everything, to be aware that I cannot control everything.

My ability to choose my response is not the only factor in getting the result I want. But it's my best shot. When I understand this truth and exercise it, I don't feel out of control. I feel in control of my experience.

Self-empowerment without humility is a wreckless wagon that will only break down in time. This is what I want to bring through my work to willing people."

The women continue to share their thoughts, and Surya is diligently listening and recording their conversation. He thanks everyone and leaves the call.

An hour before he goes to bed, Surya meditates and commits that until such an education can be a reality for all the children, he will work with as many parents as possible. He also commits that he will offer the presentation on the mind to the schools where he is helping the students learn life skills.

And before he does any of that, he will consult with experts in the field from India and elsewhere in the world and make sure his write-up and approach to coach people are qualified. Surya opens his computer and types "practical recommendations" at the end of his paper.

How do you determine what is practical?

8

When does a person change?

Antonio drives Alexa to her friend Amber's home. The boy who keeps asking Alexa out for dinner lives next door to Amber. In one of his previous visits to Amber's house, the boy gave his phone number to Alexa. Alexa promptly handed it to her mom and dad.

"Papi! Somehow, he knows each time I go to Amber's home, then shows up a few minutes after I arrive," Alexa shares.

"I understand it is bothering. I was a boy, dear. At this age, boys tend to do such things and not think about how it is for the girls. He has not done anything other than asking you for dinner, correct? Don't worry."

Victor Valdes greets Antonio and Alexa when they arrive. Victor looks majestic. He is well built and neatly groomed. He is an information technology entrepreneur. His company has built some well-known computer programs used by many retail and investment banks in the United States, Canada, Mexico, Germany, and the UK in Europe. His team has successfully delivered industry wide, standalone products, in addition to many customize built applications for their clients. With his endless enthusiasm and hard work, whatever he touches turns to gold.

After the girls go to Amber's room, Victor makes coffee for Antonio and himself. They spend time catching up on a variety of subjects. After a while, Victor asks Antonio, "My friend! Is there anything on your mind? You look like you are seriously thinking about something."

"Yes, Victor," and Antonio explains the purpose of his visit, to meet the boy.

"Boys," sighs Victor. "Being attracted is fine and completely normal. I don't like the boy lying to me about why he wants to see Amber. He claims it's to clarify his doubts from classwork, but I know better. I don't like that!"

"Isn't that how we were, Victor?" smiles Antonio.

"Yes. So what? We still have to tell him to stop stalking our daughters."

"Believe me, Victor. That's why I have come here. At the same time, I want to approach him with kindness." Antonio says very gently.

The doorbell rings. Antonio motions to Victor that he will get the door.

The boy is tall, handsome, and has searching eyes.

"Son, how can I help you?"

"I want some help from Amber…."

"Antonio, Antonio Roberto Limon!" Antonio cheerfully extends his hand and introduces himself. The boy shakes hands with Antonio with a lot of hesitation.

"Amber is with her friend right now. Come take a seat with us. Have a cup of coffee, and we will call for Amber." Antonio genuinely invites the boy in.

Jorge is bewildered. However, he obliges and follows Antonio.

Antonio plays the perfect host. He hands Jorge a plate of biscotti and coffee. Victor shakes his head in disbelief and asks Antonio and Jorge to excuse him as he has things to tend to. Antonio smiles and nods. The boy smiles nervously and bids goodbye to Victor.

"So, Jorge! How have you been."

The boy is visibly more nervous.

"How do you know my name? I have not told you yet."

"Alexa told me about you. I'm her father," Antonio smiles warmly.

The boy wants to run. Antonio gently places his hand on the boy's shoulder and asks him not to worry. Antonio's calm demeanor pacifies the boy, and he sits a bit more comfortably.

"I'm sorry, sir. I did not mean to…"

"Ask my daughter for dinner?" Antonio still smiles warmly.

"My son! Don't apologize because you think you are caught. And you don't need to say you did not mean to do something when you are afraid of the consequence. You did want to go to dinner with Alexa, didn't you?"

"Yes."

"And… what else?"

"That's all, sir, nothing else."

"I was like you, many years ago, son. Did your voice sound the same a year or two ago?"

"No, Sir."

"Did you want to go to dinner with any girl a year or two ago?"

"No."

"Do you know what has changed?" Antonio softens his voice even more.

Jorge lowers his head and keeps silent.

Antonio turns on the smart TV and picks a video from his collection on YouTube. He asks the boy if he would mind watching a fifteen-minute video. Jorge is bewildered but answers that he would not mind. There was pin-drop silence in the room for the next fifteen minutes except for the TV's audio.

Victor joined them as well a couple minutes after the video started playing.

The speaker beautifully addresses the changes boys go through in puberty. He suggests practical ways of how a boy can adapt emotionally to the changes in his body. The speaker also shares how to develop conscious thinking about puberty to avoid excessive interest in females and shame about such an interest.

Jorge was uncomfortable at first. But he was also captivated by the content and by the delivery of the speech.

All three are quiet for a while after the video. Antonio breaks the silence.

"Jorge? How do you feel?"

After a long silence, Jorge speaks.

"Umm, I don't know what to say. I feel shy and also feel relieved. I want to apologize to Amber for lying that I needed help from her for the classwork. And I will apologize to Alexa for repeatedly asking her out when she does not show interest."

"Okay then. I will let the girls know you want to have a few words with them."

Victor starts to warm up with Jorge. They both engage in a conversation about sports, how the last soccer world cup was, and what could have Mexico done better, etc.

Antonio comes back and informs Jorge that he can talk to the girls. Jorge excuses himself from Victor and leaves the room. After five minutes, he comes back to the living room, thanks Antonio, and leaves.

"He did not apologize to me for lying to my daughter and me," Victor says jokingly.

"He needs some more time and experience, Victor," Antonio says seriously.

"It's a great step already. Look, I already like the guy," says Victor.

"Ha ha. Good, good, good."

Amber and Alexa come running to the living room.

"Papi! What did you do? I could not believe my eyes and ears," says Alexa.

"I didn't do much, honey. Jorge came to his own realization after I shared an excellent video by an honest and talented speaker. Tell me! What are you girls up to?

"I've been writing a Sci-fi novel, uncle. Alexa has been helping me since last week. It is so exciting. The plot is developing much better. I love working with Alexa," says Amber.

Alexa chuckles, "Except when we fight for our idea to prevail over each other in some chapters."

"Hey! What is the fun if there is no disagreement? Working together will get very boring if there is no difference in opinion," says Victor. Antonio nods in agreement.

"Alexa, Papi has some work. I will finish and pick you up in four hours." Antonio kisses everyone goodbye and departs.

Victor is thinking about himself and how easily he gives up on people, especially where Antonio does not. Victor always evaluated his friend as generous and therefore had a blind spot. 'Generous people are also naïve,' according to Victor.

But Antonio asserts he would rather be naive than turn into a cynic, losing his faith in humanity, suspecting everyone, and trusting no one.

Victor knows he is successful in business with his approach to the world and people. He does not believe anyone quickly. In fact, a few years ago, he was always suspicious of everyone.

Victor became suspicious after a few betrayals by people at his work. Turning suspicious of everyone did not help his cause of success either. Thankfully Antonio walked into Victor's life one fine day when they were paired to play golf. It was a chance event when Antonio was offered to play as an invitation to join the club.

It is effortless to be friends with Antonio. He is lovely to talk to. He listens patiently and innocently. With no concern about his innocence, he expresses his views freely and asks questions. Victor found a breather in his life, thanks to Antonio. Gradually Victor relaxed and changed from suspecting everyone to only maintaining a healthy suspicion supported by factual information. In the past seven years, he grew his business multiple times over, thanks to the changes in his decisions since Antonio became his friend.

"Girls! I am a terrible cook. Illeana won't come back until late tonight. Shall we go to a restaurant for lunch?" Victor asks the girls.

"No, Papi! That will take too long. We could go to the food court in the mall, grab a quick bite, and return to work. I would prefer that. What do you say, Alexa?" Amber asks.

"Yes! I agree. Uncle, let's do that!"

They hop in the car and drive to the mall nearby. It's a multistory building with a cinema hall. Although it resembles modern day malls in many developed parts of the world, it still carries a Mexican touch. The colors used in the stores and throughout the mall, the warmth of the people, and Mexican paintings account for the native touch.

At the table, Alexa starts talking about the "Star Trek - Deep Space Nine" television series that she is watching with her mom. Victor and Amber excitedly comment on the episodes that Alexa says she likes very much.

"It was a crappy morning for me. I spoke to a man who bored me to death."

It is a familiar voice. Alexa catches it first, followed by Victor and Amber. It is Jorge's. He is sitting two tables away.

"Haha! What did you do?" one of his friends he is dining with asks.

"He showed me a video and hoped that I would change."

"Change to what?"

"Stop following his daughter and her friend. The friend's father is even worse. He is a dumb wit, such a fool."

Victor wants to walk up to the boys' table and punch Jorge in his face. Amber senses her father's anger and holds his hand tight. "Wait! Papi!"

"Tell me! Are they pretty? The girl and her friend. Forget the father." Another boy jumps.

"Not so pretty. They look just average. I just didn't want them to complain to my parents. My father would beat the hell out of me if they did. I went and apologized to the girls but didn't mean it. Why does it matter? Look, one day, I am going to grow bigger than my father, then he won't be able to beat me. He's going to be afraid of me." Jorge smiles with contempt.

"It ain't worth it if they're not pretty." The others laugh, and Jorge joins them.

Amber and Alexa feel a bit hurt that Jorge said they weren't pretty. At the same time, they are deeply wounded that his apology was not sincere. Amber was planning to invite him into their Sci-fi project, knowing Jorge's interests in graphic design.

Alexa is worried about how Antonio would feel when he comes to know that his little treatment or practical therapy session didn't work. Victor is fuming, but he controls himself as he does not want to do anything to the boys while the girls are around.

"God! Let me not lose faith in people again," says Victor audibly.

"Come, Papi! Let's go!"

They don't feel like eating but don't throw out and waste the food. They pack the remainder and sluggishly walk to their car.

Once they get home, the girls don't feel like writing. Victor doesn't feel like working either. But he wants to cheer the girls up. His suggestion to do a bit of work in their garden and cut the grass is received. They gradually engage themselves in the task, and time passes by.

After a couple of hours, they could hear Jorge's voice. He is getting dropped off by his friends.

Amber could not control herself. She raises her voice, "Do not ever come to our home. I thought we could be friends and that we could even work together."

Jorge lowers his head and slowly walks into his home. He noticed them when they were leaving the food court.

"Good, honey! You said what you wanted to. I am proud of you! Just leave it at that. Don't engage him by criticizing or fighting him from now on." Victor suggests.

"Okay, Dad. I won't."

Antonio brings them all dinner. "Victor! I forgot today is Wednesday. In fifteen minutes, Naren will call for the meeting I set up to introduce you to each other. Do you mind if we take it in your reading room?" Antonio asks.

"Not at all," says Victor.

"Could we also join the meeting? I would love to see and talk to Uncle Naren a bit if that is okay," Alexa excitedly asks. Alexa and Amber noticed how Neha and Kamali call adult friends of their fathers and mothers, 'Uncle.' Since then, they started doing so as well.

They all enjoy the dinner and settle in for the call.

"What technology, man! I am so many miles away, and I see you all as if you are next to me. How are all of you?" Naren never stops marveling at the technology.

"Yes, Uncle. It feels you are just next door to us. We are well. We just had an eventful day," Alexa says.

"Tell me," Naren engages Alexa. That is the only thing needed for Alexa to elaborate on everything. Antonio hears the rest of the story at the food court.

"Disappointing! I am very upset about how the boy behaved." Victor does not hesitate to express his pain and anger. Antonio is thinking.

"Girls! It is possible that Jorge is protective of you and that he cares for you," says Naren.

"What? He insulted us that we are not pretty. And he insulted our fathers," Amber sputters.

"I think, maybe, he does not want his friends to come after you. Someday sooner than later, the boys will know how pretty you are. They keep visiting Jorge's home, isn't it? With that in mind, Jorge might have known his friends would call him on his lie that you are not pretty. Yet he said so to his friends anyway. Why?" asks Naren.

"Well, maybe actually he does think we are not pretty," says Alexa.

"I like Margaret Wolfe Hungerford's words - Beauty is in the eye of the beholder. At the same time, many of us *beholders* don't deny that there is also a universal nature to beauty. That is, a majority of people agree on what is beautiful".

"Then I'm confused; why did he need to tell his friends what he thought about our fathers and us?"

"I think he is in between his decision, whether to change or not. Right or wrong, good or bad, those he was talking to in the food court are his friends! If I were him, I wouldn't want to part with my friends and deal with the consequences. At his age, in his mind, he needs to prove that he's a man, tough, etc. So, he starts a conversation where he tells how he is dismissive of all of you; dads and daughters. Do you have any idea of how his parents are with him?"

"I don't know about his mom. But Jorge said that his father would beat the hell out of him if he came to know what Jorge wanted from Alexa."

Naren concludes his observation. "It makes sense to me why Jorge is possibly the way he is. In any case, you can just observe. I have faith that he will leave his bad company and come to you for another apology. When he does that, he will not change his stand for fear of losing friends."

"I believe in humanity and Jorge," says Antonio serenely.

"Jorge coming to a decision to change maybe soon, or it might take a long time, or it might never happen, but we can keep the faith that one can change. At the same time, we can remain cautious, not open flood gates with our sympathy or happiness when we are praised," Naren shares.

"Come on, Uncle! So, are we pretty?" Amber chuckles.

"Does it matter? When the person I have grown to dislike suggests that I am not pretty, why do I still bother? We are so fixated that we should be seen as pretty girls. That is too much pressure. I'm going to stop playing the game," Alexa answers.

"Me too," says Antonio. "I color my beard black. I want to be seen as young."

"There is my honest Antonio. I will follow suit, I do too," says Victor.

"Does it mean we shouldn't care about how we look when we go out, and we should not care when we are indoors?" Amber asks.

"I don't think it means that, honey. It's nice and feels good to groom ourselves. It's when we become obsessive about how we look that narcissism can enter our lives," says Ileana, who has been standing by the side of the room, waiting to enter the conversation.

"Mom! We missed you," Amber runs to Ileana and hugs her.

"What is your take on narcissism, Aunty? I have read stories about it, but I want to understand it more in depth," says Alexa.

"Why don't we keep it for some other day? I promise we will talk about it within the next week." Ileana hugs Alexa and leads everyone to the dining table.

Would you stop doing what you believe is the right thing to do if you didn't get the result you wanted?

9

World 2050

Pat arrived in New York City last night via interstate highway I-87. Not minding the free breakfast provided in the hotel at which he stayed, Pat is on the road again this morning. He is on I-95, another interstate highway, from New York City to Edison, New Jersey. Pat always enjoys the local roads, which celebrates his nostalgia for old, narrow, tree-lined roads on each side, little towns that pass by, and the ease with which he can pull over to a diner and have a meal.

On this trip however, Pat wanted to find how the highways are for a specific reason. He finds them efficient and sterile, and the drive boring after a while.

He misses his friends he grew up with in Boston. They had many laughs together in their younger years, rendered shoulders to each other when in pain, and parted with sorrowful smiles as they or their families moved to pursue opportunities elsewhere. Pat moved to upstate New York two decades ago. As he drives, his mind is also traveling - down memory lane.

He watched a fictionalized documentary – India 2050, from Discovery Plus - India edition after Naren told him about it. If Indians continue to live the way they do, how will the country and living conditions look in 2050?' There is also a glimpse and representation of life in New York City, drawn in parallel, in one of the scenes.

The projected consequences to human life in 2050 in the documentary due to our mishandling of resources was shocking, to say the least. He wondered whether he avoided seeing what his fellow humans have been doing to the environment. Hence Pat decided to use the highways on this trip.

Pat usually drives down the Taconic State Parkway to go back and forth from New York City. The scenery is colorful in all seasons except in the winter. Pat finds even the winter drive to be beautiful and a reminder of the green that will follow in the Spring, helping to be grateful to nature's offerings.

He wonders how his father and grandfather would have felt about these changes in their time to the neighborhood, roadways, and environment.

'In comparison to India, the United States has better water availability for all its population. The projection that 40 percent of India's population might not have access to water by 2050 was particularly disturbing. Would the United States face such a problem? Even if it is not 40 percent of the population, 10 percent of the people not having access to water might result in civil strife. What can I do to help my people? What can Naren do in India? Shall I ask him to move to a different country?'

Pat's mind is continuously churning thoughts, running much faster than his truck. He decides to take the next exit from the highway and drive down the local road for the rest of the journey. After taking the exit, he stops for a meal by the first diner he encounters.

As he walks in, Pat remembers that a precursor to all diners, the first one was created in Providence, Rhode Island, in 1872. *'This one still looks like a diner,'* Pat muses. He finds a quiet booth and settles in. He orders a garden omelet with home fries and whole wheat toast. The waiter attending to Pat is an elderly gentleman in his late eighties. He brings a pot of coffee to Pat.

"How do you know I like coffee?" Pat is surprised.

"I lived long enough to spot a man who likes coffee, young man!" the man grinned happily.

"Billy! If you want to rest for a while, feel free." A woman in her mid-fifties speaks warmly as she walks by.

"Oh! Don't you worry, my dear! I can work all this week without having to sleep." Billy responds cheerfully.

It is a 24-hour diner.

"We had a hectic morning. Billy was so busy that he got to eat only half an hour ago," the lady explains to Pat, who is intently watching both of them.

It is heartwarming to converse with humble, down to earth people. Pat can find many such folks from the countryside. The cities are a different story for Pat. That is why Pat turned down any opportunity, however lucrative it was, to work and live in big cities. Pat has a few friends who love city life. They call him to join them all the time.

'People make the difference, whether in the city or countryside. At the same time, most people who want peace will move to the countryside. The pace of interactions in a city sets up the mind to be agitated, at least for me.' Pat thinks.

'What would happen to this Diner in 2050? Who would be running it? Would it even exist? Will people go out to eat, or will they get everything delivered to their homes?' The scene from the 2050 video where the narrator says she eats only one cooked meal a day and relies on pills for the rest of the time comes to his mind. An involuntarily shiver passes through his body for a moment.

Billy gently asks, "Are you cold, my friend? I can turn down the air conditioner for you."

"No Billy, thank you. I'm alright. Why don't you grab a seat? I could use some company," says Pat.

"Thank you…."

"My name is Patrick Williams."

"Good name. I'm William Madison. Pat, I'll bring your food and sit with you. Thank you."

"The pleasure is mine, Billy."

Billy quickly returns with the food and artfully serves it. Pat instantly learns he is watching an honest worker who respects and loves his job.

"You are an artist!" exclaims Pat.

"Thank you, Pat. I love serving food." Billy smiles and sits opposite Pat. He pours himself a cup of coffee, does not add sugar, and slowly sips the hot liquid.

"You mind if I ask you how old you are?"

"Not at all; I am eighty-nine and will turn ninety in two months."

Pat is happy that Billy is agile and active. It reminds him of his grandmother, who was very active until she passed away at ninety-five.

"What is bothering you, young man?" Billy asks.

"I guess there is no point asking how you knew something is bothering me, mind reader!" Pat laughs and continues, "I watched a documentary last night. If we all continue to live the way we mainly do now and spend the resources of our planet the way we do, where we end up is not going to be a pretty place."

"Hmm! That could keep you awake at night."

"It does."

"You know, Pat, when I was driving to work this morning, I saw a billboard which read, 'Save the planet.' I was laughing. 'From whom?' The real deal is 'Save us humans, from us, isn't it? The planet is fine. It will take care of itself. Perhaps the planet is responding to our actions of extracting way more than we need and affecting other lives."

"True!" Pat nods in agreement.

"I have grandkids, Billy! I'm concerned about how their lives will be when they grow up!"

"I feel you! These days if I talk about such things, people tell me I'm depressed and ask me if I have anything fun to talk about. I am not against fun. In fact, most of the time, I joke around. There are a few times, I feel I must bring some sense into people. But people are very blind, Pat! Very blind and deaf, too!"

"Yeah! Sadness is something most people don't want to feel. They're willing to feel upset and depressed if they don't get what they want. But they don't take time to notice the difficulties in others' lives.

How many animals are ruthlessly slaughtered each day? How many trees are needlessly uprooted? We wipe out the ecosystem to just get what we want."

"Oh, Pat! You understand the problem very well. All the activists are going after industrialists and politicians. Instead, they all should go to the public and make a plea to curb needless consumption altogether.

I have a car that's been running for 30 years. Except for some minor repairs here or there, it's in good order, you know! It passed the government's inspection too. Look, the number of cars in America, old and new, will surpass our entire population by 2 or 3 times, I think. And it's not that every person has a car; I read somewhere 863 out of every 1000 of us have a car.

People who can afford to, keep replacing their cars quickly, and there is a growing population of available cars for purchase, new and old. We keep buying them, leasing them, and changing them according to our whim and fancy."

Billy pauses a bit and continues.

"Pat, my son! I am not saying that we should not advance technologically, but where is our focus?

Technological advances can be used to address so many causes. Our car manufacturers could spend their time collaborating with other manufacturers in other countries and make better products for people who don't have cars. Instead, they keep selling to the same population, promoting their good, better, and the best cars.

If all the consumers open their eyes and hearts and see the problems plaguing the environment and the other people, they will not indulge in needless purchases. And when the behaviors in consumers change, industrialists will look at other ways and means of earning their profits.

Look, Pat, we live in a world where maybe 10 to 20 percent of people think the way we do. Out of them, maybe 2 or 3 percent take consistent actions for change. At the same time, there is potential, as if turning a switch, if every one of us sets our mind that we don't want things we don't need. When we do that, all these 'save the planet' problems are solved."

"But how is that possible? Even people living under the same roof don't agree with each other."

"Well, not when it comes to survival. We're getting to that inevitability."

"What do you mean, Billy?"

"When we do things out of love, care, and enthusiasm, we progress and we evolve. When we do things out of fear where we have nothing to be afraid of, then we consume everything on the planet in a frenzy."

Pat looks at Billy with a question in his eyes as Billy continues to speak.

"Our survival instinct is turned against us by ourselves accidentally. Then it is fueled by profit-oriented people who do not care about the expense to others."

"I don't understand."

"I am going to read a couple of paragraphs to you; one moment, please." Billy walks to the counter and comes back with his bag. He opens a vintage notebook and flips the pages. He stops at a page and starts reading a note, which is in his own handwriting.

"*Now, why is there the desire to fulfill oneself? Obviously, the desire to fulfill, to become something, arises when there is awareness of being nothing. I think I'm nothing because I'm insufficient, empty, inwardly poor; I struggle to become something; outwardly or inwardly, I struggle to fulfill myself with another person, in a thing, through an idea.* **To fill that imaginary void is the whole process of our existence.** *By telling ourselves that we are empty, we struggle either to collect things outwardly or to cultivate inward riches. When there is an understanding of 'what is,' which is emptiness and inward insufficiency, and when one lives with that insufficiency and understands it fully, there comes creative reality and creative intelligence, which alone brings happiness.*"

Pat listens to Billy attentively. He is understanding something but not completely. "You wrote this, Billy?"

"No, Pat. A long many years ago, I attended a talk given by the man who spoke these words. These words pierced me, and I wrote these down in my notebook. *His name is Jiddu Krishnamurti.* I met him when I was traveling in California. A dear friend of mine, Kimberley, invited me to attend a talk with her. I had no idea what it was about at the time. It was a pleasant evening, and I felt good around many friendly people I saw there.

Then came the speaker, affectionately called JK. He was unassuming, simple, and elegant. He is probably the kindest man I have ever seen to date. People asked him questions, and he, in turn, helped us understand our own questions through dialogue.

He spoke about an imaginary void for which he gave a name - 'inward insufficiency.' Mind you, it is not a real thing! It's in our imagination that we are empty, and we think we need something to fill the emptiness and make us complete. The imagination is a label to a feeling.

Now, let me elaborate that a little bit so that I can be clear. How do we know we are hungry, or what is hunger? It's a sensation, right? Unlike hunger, which is connected to an activity such as eating, this feeling or sensation JK gives a name to as inward insufficiency is not connected to any physical activity by its Nature. But we associate it with different things and feel satisfied only when we get those things – such as a house, jewelry, maybe a husband or a wife, words of acceptance or a hug, whatever."

Pat is still not fully understanding what Billy is explaining. But as he listens, it makes more sense. Each sentence spoken by Billy better clarifies the meaning of the previous sentence. So, Pat decides to listen to Billy completely before asking a question or making a comment.

Billy continues. "Do you remember the story of Alexander the Great?"

"Yes. The Greek king who died at the young age of 32 and already known as the undefeated conqueror. If I remember what I read about him in my history book correctly, he built one of the largest empires stretching from Greece to northwestern India. He made all his conquests just after he came to the throne at the age of 20."

"Good. You remember correctly. What do you think might have been his motivation?"

"To be the greatest king, to have the largest kingdom?"

Billy reads a line from those two paragraphs. *"I am aware of my insufficiency, my inward poverty, and I struggle to run away from it or to fill it."*

And he continues to speak. "Our motivations are all feelings. We experienced motivation before we knew any words and when we were babies. When the stomach is empty, it's a physical thing. It feels empty, and we don't like it.

The sensation and feeling of emptiness drive me to go for food. It's an instinct. Are you with me?"

"Yes," says Pat. He forgets the food and listens even more attentively.

"What if there is a feeling that is intense like hunger, but food does not quench it? Alexander thought kingdoms would fulfill his imaginary appetite. Unlike food, even though a kingdom is a physical thing, it is not something you can eat away." Billy laughs and continues.

"So, the imaginary appetite is seemingly satisfied for a moment. And Alexander probably started another conquest when he thought he was insufficient.

Basically, the mind creates a fiction about a feeling and says one needs to do something about it. This feeling is somewhat similar to how it feels when you are terribly hungry or alone in a dark alley. For lack of better words, let me say that it is a feeling that is disturbing and highly uncomfortable."

"Okay, I'm getting it, Billy."

"Good. Good! The human body goes through so many different experiences, perhaps even starting in the womb and then on its way out.

Who knows what feelings or sensations are caused by what? Does it even matter?" Billy pauses for a bit and continues.

"It does. It matters for the mind since we were babies. The mind, perhaps, is designed to protect the body and to look for comfort or pleasure. It is essential to do so for the survival and extension of a species into the future.

In the infantile stages, the mind concludes any uncomfortable feeling needs to be resolved. A physical issue such as hunger, can be resolved. But how can an imaginary issue be truly resolved? How can you delete one sensation you don't like?

When you think tangible or intangible things are needed from others and the environment to resolve the disturbing feeling, it never works because our imagination is like a black hole. It can consume the entire universe, and it would not be enough.

Since the meeting, I understood that the continuous indulgence in comfort and pleasure makes us dull and insensitive to other lives and our own. It blocks us from being able to think.

So, we justify in order to indulge. Indulgence helps in some ways. Take an alcoholic, for example. Sometimes, they forget any pain with the intake of alcohol.

The general population indulges in seemingly innocuous ways, such as food. And we create several reasons to justify eating. Then we run to dieticians, nutritionists, etc. But until we attend to why we overdo anything, we will create a plethora of needless methods and industries to control our habits. I am not against all those who make a living out of advising others what to eat. I only think if we become a bit more conscious, we can all have more meaningful work and time in the world."

"I understand and agree. So, we are all good story writers. When there is an unsettling feeling, we write a story that we need something to settle it."

"Yes, Pat. At the very least, if we are aware that we are serving a feeling, half the problem we created for ourselves is solved. Instead, we incorrectly think we are settled or unsettled upon experiencing feelings. There is a gulf of difference between being aware that 'I feel settled/unsettled,' vs. 'I am settled/unsettled.'

Fundamentally, even the term 'unsettling' is nothing but describing and assigning a word, an abstraction, to an experience. A feeling is a physical sensation. And we define for ourselves based on our experiences of which sensations are okay to bear and which are not. The feelings we don't want to experience are labeled as unsettling. Your mind makes your body feel 'settled' after it acquires what it thinks is needed to create another feeling which is either pleasant or tolerable. It's all fiction. Most of the time, we believe we're going after something else, like if I buy a house with a garage, a car, and I have a family, then I achieve the American dream. I'm a complete man. But it doesn't end there, does it?"

"It does not."

"Correct. We don't stop eating until we die or until we can't eat due to an illness, right?"

"Hmm."

"But unlike the necessity of food, many things that we think are needed to make us feel settled aren't. Until we understand this deeply in our hearts and gut, we will run after things and destroy everything along our path, whether we intended or not." Billy continues.

"JK said another thing. Thought identifies itself with that sensation, and through identification, the 'I,' the ego, is built up, and then the ego says, 'I must,' or 'I will not.' It's in our language. When I feel hungry, a sensation, I say I'm hungry, isn't it so?

We also do the same with ideas. The American home is an idea. It's not a physical thing. If I don't have 'The American home,' I don't feel settled, and I think I'm not complete. The problem continues."

Pat speaks. "When I feel extreme hunger, everything else of any importance gets set aside unless I collect myself. I think that's what we do when we think we need something, for which the tragic result is we wreak havoc on the planet. So, Billy? What is the solution?"

"I think one of the key solutions is to bring this awareness to each and every person possible. The mere observation and total attention to this feeling, and any other feelings in our body, with no judgment, dissolves it. JK spent all his life to bring this capacity of total attention to all people, in my opinion. And I can speak from my experience that it works. As the whole population gains this awareness, little by little problems will subside."

Pat shares. "There is a contemporary Indian Guru who says the famous avatar Krishna attempted to spiritualize politics. He attempted to bring spirituality to the top leadership - the kings - so that it will pass down to all else in their kingdom. But he failed. No one listened to him."

Billy says, "At the top level, it's a tough call unless we have a few sensible leaders. I think most people at the top are there propelled by a desire. Not to say there aren't those at the top that endeavor to live up to their responsibility, but it's not always the primary driver for their motivation."

"Well, we need a **Statue of Responsibility**. Someone, a famous author or a speaker, said that. Just as we have a **Statue of Liberty** on the east coast, we need one for Responsibility on the west coast, so that America is balanced," Pat says.

"That was *Viktor Frankl.* I guess you don't know."

"I don't know what?"

"There is a project that will bring the Statue of Responsibility to the west coast in 2023. It is honoring Viktor Frankl."

Pat looks in disbelief.

"For real, check the internet," says Billy. He also scribbles the name of the website, statueofresponsibility.com, and gives it to Pat.

Pat feels like a humble and thankful student would, to a generous and kind teacher.

"Billy, you should be a counselor or a teacher."

"You take that job, young man! I love waiting tables and talking to beautiful souls like you."

The lady walks by and shakes hands with Pat, saying, "All friends of Billy are friends of mine."

"Yes, you are my friend and a teacher. Thank you, Billy."

Billy walks with Pat to the truck. Pat starts his truck with a renewed sense of hope and a big smile. There are caring people like Billy in the world. Pat waves a grateful thanks to Billy.

That night, he visits the website Billy told him about, and finds the following:

"Freedom is in danger of degenerating into mere arbitrariness unless it is lived in terms of responsibleness. That is why I recommend that the Statue of Liberty on the East Coast be supplemented by a Statue of Responsibility on the West Coast."

-Dr. Viktor E. Frankl

Pat continues to read the mission of the creators of the project. *"The Statue of Responsibility Foundation™ consists of individuals who are dedicated to realizing Viktor Frankl's vision. Our mission is to positively and significantly alter society's sense of Responsibility to itself and its communities by demonstrating that Liberty and Responsibility are INSEPARABLE ideals. Not only is Responsibility a necessary condition for a free society to prosper, it will move individuals to aspire to their highest potential."*

"I wish them my very best and will extend my hands. May their intent succeed in the world!" Pat writes in his journal before he sleeps.

Should we increase or reduce the number of things for which we are responsible?

10

Personal Reasons!

Naren finished the call with his client, Will Rodgers.

'There is more than one way to say a thing to appeal to the listener.' Naren finds this statement almost always true. Ultimately the listener's willingness to hear what the speaker says is the only key. What makes one willing? The person themself. And a caring person often works to find and communicate in the language of the listener so that the idea stands a chance of consideration.

Naren needs to work hard with many people, but Will is not one of them. When what he hears does not appeal immediately to him, Will focuses hard and makes sure he understands the subject. Naren came across an article about fasting from dopamine. *Dopamine is a type of neurotransmitter. Your body makes it, and your nervous system uses it to send messages between nerve cells. That's why it's sometimes called a chemical messenger. Dopamine plays a role in how we feel pleasure. Source: webmd.com*

The write-up helped Naren to explain how Will's addiction to food has affected his senses and wanting or craving. Let's consider the case of a person who likes chocolate very much and is addicted to it. The person can easily access a chocolate, and they do not miss a chance to eat as much as they can every time.

What happens? The taste buds will get blunt over time. Now they need to eat more to feel the taste. And a person seeking pleasure most of the time will have low pain tolerance. Naren understood these concepts that are well explained in the article, with which he made the conversation with Will effective.

Will understood what he had been doing to his body. Other than this one area of his life, Will is a very successful man. He is loved by his family, respected by his clients, and adored by his employees.

Will has an impeccable work ethic and is a caring father to his six kids. He is often asked by his community to teach teenagers practical skills.

Will dropped out of school when he was thirteen. His love for buildings propelled his career to a new high. At the young age of twenty, he grew his family construction business' revenue from one million to five million dollars a year. He never hesitates to get his hands dirty with manual labor or to draw a blueprint himself. He has the elegance and etiquette to deal with his wealthy clients, play golf with them, dine with them, and do presentations that get them immediately engaged. At the same time, he is simple, unassuming, and he loves to sit and share a meal as often as he can with his employees who do hard labor.

Will is six and a half feet tall and weighs two hundred and fifty pounds. Lately, he is bothered by his excess weight. He's offered a session at the local 'Youth Development Group' to teach youngsters' goal setting in their most challenging area. Will almost rejected the offer as he is not making progress in his own challenging area. His wife, Kathy, encouraged him to use this as an opportunity to work on his ideal weight goal.

Will knows how big the weight-loss industry is. He believes the industry is as big as it is today because of a lack of permanent solutions to why one puts on weight. He did not want to go to a trainer who teaches a technique but rather to someone who understands him well. So, he chose Naren, and they had their call this morning. Naren helped Will understand how addiction works, quoting excerpts from the 'detox article.'

When Will asked how to work on his addiction to eating, Naren asked in turn what Will's reasons to achieve an ideal body weight are? Will explained the offer to teach the kids in his community about achieving a goal in an area they are challenged. Will added he didn't think it was right for him to go as the speaker who does not walk the talk.

Naren asked him whether there were any other difficult areas where Will achieved his goals. Will recognized that when he has the interest and willingness, working on a goal in a difficult subject is just a matter of taking practical, necessary steps. And he has done that in many areas of his life.

Naren suggested reading the book, *'Man's Search for Meaning'* by Victor Frankl. He also asked Will to think about why he would not consider how he mastered other challenging areas of his life to support his position as the speaker who does walk the talk.

'Does Will need to succeed in every goal to be the presenter? What if he shares with the kids how he still is challenged in some areas, and that will help them understand that there are challenges throughout life? Success in an area does not end the journey but makes a person more equipped to handle another area.'

Will sets an appointment to meet Naren after two days. Then he goes to the local bookstore right away to buy the suggested Victor Frankl book, a timeless piece of work.

Naren walks to Kamali, who is getting ready for her singing lesson through Skype.

"What is your most difficult area, honey?"

"Why are you asking this now, Pa?"

"I'm helping a friend who is also my client, Kamali! And I want to know how you manage your difficult objectives. Maybe it can help me improve my methods!"

"Haha. I usually take a break, Dad. Then I go and do something fun. After some time, when I try to do the difficult thing, it's not as hard."

"Good deal, Kamali! Thank You!"

Kamali did not say anything that Naren didn't know. What she said, however, reminded him of the thing adults forget most of the time. Naren sometimes forgets, and he recognizes most of his clients also forget to take short breaks during the day. As adults, we like to worry and sit on the same thing instead of relaxing the mind. We've gone many days like this before realizing it, then we tell ourselves we need a vacation.

It's a common trend to say to oneself and others that 'I choose everything, and I can change my thoughts, emotions, and actions.' It is genuinely empowering when one is actually able to change them at will. It is crippling, though, to say it when one is not able to do so.

Naren finds that in comparison to thoughts and emotions, actions are easy to change. Naren thinks, "Until one creates the flexibility to pause and choose thoughts and emotions, a person lying that they are able to choose those modalities at will disempowers themself immediately."

A child is usually honest. He/she just does what is possible and does not create guilt about where he/she fails. Naren pays a lot of attention to this aspect of Kamali's growth and maturity. He makes sure Kamali does not create unnecessary guilt or worry about her capabilities and allows her to be flexible in her own ways to find a solution for her challenges.

"Well, it is time for me to take a break," Naren says to himself. Naren rests on the easy-chair, one of his grandfather's collections and gifts. He closes his eyes and reduces all the activity of his thoughts. Soon he enters a deep state of inaction, inactivity, and steps further and further into it. He is not asleep but in a condition close to sleep with his awareness intact.

Naren is able to achieve such a state after many years of practice. A monk once told him when a person is committed to being in a monastery, they can reach such a state within months. Once frustrated about his pace, Naren came to terms with what was possible for him and found his zone at his pace. It was after sixteen years of practice.

Uma is keen on her work. She is a leader of a seven-member development team. The seven, including Uma, have solved many problems that were left as unsolvable by the rest of the organization. The team is modeled after Uma's patience and tenacity. They don't give up easily. Uma is 100% focused on what she does. Yet, each day, when it is 5 pm, like the precision of her Swiss-made watch, she walks to the kitchen, makes coffee for her and Naren, and prepares a light snack for Kamali.

"Mom! Look at this! Come on!" Kamali exclaims from where she is.

"Give me a sec, honey!" Uma walks to Naren, gently taps him, and hands him the coffee.

"What should I look at?" Uma lovingly asks an excited Kamali.

Kamali removes the thin towel, which she used to cover her pencil sketch.

"Oh my! That looks like a black and white photograph!"

Kamali proudly giggles and says, "Thank you, Mom!"

Naren stands next to Uma, awestruck. "How long did it take, Kamali dear?"

"18 hours, Dad!"

"Brilliant!"

"Uncle Antonio was telling me about the 'photograph-like-pencil-sketch' he was making. I watched some videos on YouTube and started my sketch."

"He would love to see your work."

"I already took a photo and messaged him. I thanked him for the inspiration."

"Sweet! What next, Kamali?" asks Uma.

"I don't know! I will eat my snack and then decide."

Naren smiles and walks to the study. Taking care of Kamali is the best thing that ever happened to Naren. He considers bringing up Kamali to be the best of his ongoing achievements. She responds to his efforts and cares with an unspoken commitment. Sometimes she doesn't quite understand what Naren says. And in those instances, Naren talks to her and learns how to communicate with her such that she does.

Meanwhile, Will is deeply engrossed in the book. How Viktor Frankl, in a Nazi concentration camp, held the image of his beloved, his wife, as the subject of his contemplation and inspiration captivates Will's heart. Will understands how Viktor's act helped him in all the moments up to his survival and then after his meaningful life.

It is midnight. He looks at his beautiful wife. A woman who never says she is tired. A lovely soul that joyously gave birth to their six children. A woman who trusted the uneducated, raw Will since she was a little girl. It did not require much from Will but a few words. She was waiting for him to say those words. And they were married.

Her face absorbs the moonlight that slips through the window and retains the coolness. She has also retained a smile that says, 'I know you are watching me.'

Will continues to watch her with admiration, love, and crosses the boundary of all thoughts in his mind. Will enters a new state of togetherness. He could not quite describe the state he is experiencing if anyone were to ask.

He always concluded his best feelings and experiences are because of Kathy. And now Kathy's presence transports Will to another world, helped by Viktor Frankl's words.

Will thinks that perhaps some of the self-help book authors who proclaim a person can create whatever emotion they choose without the presence of the other, have not experienced the ever-growing depths of love. Some of those authors and speakers possibly stop at a limited depth, accidentally and unknowingly supporting narcissism in the name of empowerment.

What is life without the presence and contemplation of another, especially one's beloved? Humans need one and another. How can an individual be empowered without recognizing another's contribution in their life? How can one be empowered without any love in their heart?

'The great yogis held the image of their beloved until they attained a state they describe as 'Shiva,' from another dimension.' He remembers what he read of India's great works.

Thus, Will burns the midnight oil and beyond. He does not sleep. Kathy wakes up at five in the morning and finds Will sitting by the poolside. She walks up to him and understands she does not need to ask if he is okay. He looks serene and resolved.

When she is close, Will says, "Honey! Naren helped me arrive at an important decision."

Kathy does not ask what it is. She pays all her attention to Will and listens intently.

"Please don't make me the usual breakfast I like. I want to eat some fresh vegetables and yogurt."

Kathy nods her acknowledgment and strokes Will's hair. "Now go and sleep a bit. I will wake you up in three hours."

"Yes." Will walks to the bedroom.

Meanwhile, Naren, Uma, and Kamali are playing Carrom. They crack jokes continuously; most of the time, Naren is being made fun of.

"When are you talking to Will again?"

"We agreed after a couple of days, but I have a feeling we will be talking in the morning. I know Will. I think he already finished reading the book."

Uma acknowledges and speaks, "They have six children. Incredible! I think I can grow one more, maybe two, and that's about it."

"Kathy and Will work very hard to balance their business and family. From the time I have known them, I've seen them paying a lot of attention and care to raise their children. And they have friendly neighbors who are an extended family. If we ever live in the States, I think it would be great to move to Will's neighborhood."

"Nice. What do you guys want for dinner?"

"I will cook, Uma. What would you both like?"

"Great! Why don't you make some lentil soup and toast the bread?"

Kamali likes that choice.

And thus, Naren, Uma, and Kamali conclude their day. The next morning, Will calls Naren and says he changed his diet.

"Already?" asks Naren.

"I read the book, and I watched my lovely wife's face almost all night. I have my personal reasons to stay healthy, Naren. The book was amazing."

"That's great. We have Viktor Frankl to thank. Let's endure, my friend. The women of our homes have done a lot, a lion share of work for our families and us. A simple reflection of a few minutes would bring us close to them through gratitude and love. You know this already. I just reminded you as I reminded myself this week. That's all."

"I know what I am going to talk about in my meeting with the teenagers in our community."

"You sure do! All the best!"

"Thank you. Alright, Naren! Talk to you soon!"

"Adios amigo, bye for now."

Should you be an expert in everything you do in order to help someone improve?

11

Liberty and Responsibility

Kamali and Neha are having a discussion. Soon the discussion turns into a loud argument. Uma and Kavya walk to them and ask what their disagreement is about.

Neha tells Kavya. "We were given a topic to talk about, ma. 'Liberty and Responsibility.'"

"Okay! It's an excellent topic. What do you disagree about?" says Kavya.

"I'm saying they are two different things. Neha says they are opposite to each other," says Kamali.

"I see," says Uma.

"Ma! Our teacher wants us to find the relationship between these two concepts. Liberty is freedom. When you are responsible, you can't be as free as much. You can't do everything you want to do, right?" says Neha.

"My dad told me Liberty and Responsibility are different things, but they are not opposed to each other. When I asked him to explain, he asked me to think and discuss with Neha. We both have been arguing since we started our discussion."

"Maybe you both can do a little more work before you argue, I mean, discuss," says Uma.

"What kind of work?" asks Kamali.

"First, understand the two words. Words represent a concept. And most concepts are from actions. Even thinking is a type of activity. Why don't you both use this clue and really understand what those words mean? Then we all can sit and chat about it," says Kavya. Uma nods in agreement.

Uma and Kavya are spending time together today. Clark and Naren went for a walk in the coconut fields. After they return, they will prepare lunch. Both Naren and Clark take a keen interest in cooking and other household activities. They eagerly help their partners and, at times, surprise their wives with a new recipe or two. Thanks to YouTube channels by enthusiastic people who love to share recipes, Clark and Naren maintain an endless playlist of videos. The videos come in handy when they want to cook something new.

The kids borrowed Kavya's iPad and started studying Liberty and Responsibility, using dictionary.com and thesaurus.com. They are diligently writing down all the meanings and examples cited. Uma could hear Neha suggesting to Kamali that they now attempt to find examples from their own lives. Kavya hears too. They both are happy when their girls invest time and energy in learning new things and practicing thinking about them.

Meanwhile, Clark is informing Naren about the benefits of chewing his food 40 times. He has been diligent at it since they met the last time. When Naren says he does not chew as many times, Clark asks him why. Naren says that the objective of chewing 40 times is what he focuses on and not necessarily the number.

"I started with 40, and I soon understood that the person who instructed the others to do so would have wanted to make sure the solid food is absolutely ground into liquid. Food such as Idli (steamed rice cake) becomes absolutely liquid in less than 15 repetitions. Some other food requires 40. When I make Rotis, I would need to chew them 50 times as I still don't know how to make them smooth."

Naren laughs and continues. "I think perhaps meat products would need to be chewed 40 times. Most of the time, what I eat is already soft, and hence I modified the rule. I pay attention to the objective and stop."

"Smart thing to do," chuckles Clark. "I still follow instructions and do not evaluate each situation on its merit, particularly in this area - wellness. I just need a fitness expert telling me what to do, and I will do it without thinking!"

"Come on, don't be hard on yourself! It's an innocent approach, totally fine! I followed the instruction diligently for a couple of weeks before I adapted, remembering my objectives - good digestion, energetic body, and appropriate work distribution between my teeth and intestines. It is very easy to forget the goal and do the activity as a habit. In fact, when we are not conscious, the habits just make us robotic."

"True, the world is dynamic, constantly changing. We make it static and immovable in our minds when we forget awareness of our habits. It's similar to getting into an engineless car and expecting it to move."

"Hahaha. Well said, Clark. So, what else is new?"

"It's election time in the United States. We got some usual business, massive data entry work. For the next three months, we will be able to pay our people. I am looking for new ways for our companies to function and bring money. It's hard to find someone who loves selling."

"I know, Naren. Selling forces a change in the person, whether they want it or not. One needs to adapt and become flexible. Perhaps most of us do not want to be flexible."

"Flexibility requires effort to stop the old and begin something new. Why wouldn't it be hard?"

"Is it effort or willingness?" Naren asks.

"Willingness, which is emotional effort."

"No wonder we need a powerful enough reason or meaning for almost anything new we want to do."

"Unless it is so easy, like, lifting a finger!"

"Haha!"

After an hour of the walk, they stop by two coconut trees. Without any hesitation, they each climb a tree and fetch enough tender coconuts for everyone. Then they walk to the farmhouse.

"What do you want to cook?" Clark asks Naren.

"I am thinking of making vegetable biriyani. Do you fancy anything else?"

"That'll do. I can help make some cauliflower fry and raita for the sides."

"Great."

As soon as Clark and Naren walk into the house, Neha and Kamali run to them.

"Dad! We have been studying, discussing, and sometimes arguing about liberty and responsibility. Do you want to hear us?" Neha asks Clark while also looking at Naren.

"Honey! Would you mind discussing with your moms for now? We're going to cook some food, and in the evening, we can all sit together and talk," says Clark.

"Alright." In no time the girls are gone. They both are athletic and agile.

Uma and Kavya are relaxing in two swings and talking about different topics.

"I have been working on a sweater for a week, Kavya."

Uma extends the sweater, and Kavya looks at it with excitement. She likes how the sweater feels on her hands. When Uma says she made it for Kavya, Kavya feels even more excited.

"Thank You, Uma! How do you find time to do all this despite being a busy programmer?"

"Oh! If I don't do other things, my head will explode. For me, knitting is as important as programming, Kavya. We have made our lives so complex. Living in the countryside and growing our own food would be far better than our current lives in the city, I think. Distance lends enchantment to the view. Still, I think I would opt any day to be a farmer and deal with uncertainties in nature and animals instead of doing what I am doing. Naren is also of the same idea. At some point, we want to switch to natural lives. He likes to teach and has been applying to work in an alternate school, similar to the ones run by the Krishnamurti Foundation. And I would till the land any day."

"Sweet, Uma. That is why we have chosen this life. The clinic I have for the villagers earns me a decent amount of money, and I also offer two out of my five days to serve those who cannot afford health care. You know how much Clark likes to work in the fields. He likes his software business too. He is also at a crossroads given the level of automation in the technology industry that is gradually changing the scope of his business. The usual work that had been his company's bread and butter is getting reduced day by day."

"I love that you both live here."

"You could come more often or stay in our parents' home. They won't be back from Australia for two years."

"Really? Wow! I would love to take that offer. We're only working remotely, anyway. I'm positive that Kamali and Naren will welcome the idea as well."

"Super."

"Tell me! Are you guys planning a second child?"

"Likely, no, Uma. It's quite a responsibility to bear. And looking at how we are depleting the resources of the planet, I fear what it might be like for Kamali and Neha when they grow up."

"Naren and I feel the same. As a race, we're not able to draw a line and say what we have is enough. Many of us don't have enough nutrition, water, and sanitation. Those who don't have enough will eventually join the ones that do not stop accumulating upon finding an opportunity. It looks like to me, 'having power,' and 'safeguarding our bodies and chasing pleasurable experiences' are the only focus of more than 90% of us."

"I know. The school has given such a good topic for our children to talk about. Without responsibility, we humans abuse liberty and drive our bodies to the graveyard."

"Yes, and without liberty, responsibility becomes a burden and breaks our backs."

"Hmm, let's hear what our children have to say. I think they will bring a new light on this subject."

"I am looking forward to it. Why don't we all catch up after lunch?"

"What about inviting the men?"

"Naren and Clark wanted to go to the neighboring village to meet someone. And on their way back, they want to go for a swim in the canal."

"Okay. Very good."

Neha and Kamali are playing Carrom. Kavya and Uma join them. The men are cooking.

After a sumptuous meal, Clark and Naren depart to the neighboring village while Uma prepares a nice natural bed made of the fallen leaves. Kavya cleans all the utensils and joins Uma. When Neha and Kamali see Uma working, they help her out. The densely planted coconut trees offer a cool shelter, yet there is an adequate space to make the bed. The breeze is lovely, and they all are delighted to be in the field. Kavya joins shortly.

"So, kids, what have you come up with?"

Kamali speaks with a lot of excitement. "After a while, we stopped looking at the internet for the meaning of the words. Liberty means freedom, right? And freedom means…"

Neha jumps in quickly, "doing whatever you can and whenever! Doesn't it? But when you are responsible, you can't do whatever and whenever. So, your liberties are less."

"I see. How come?" Uma asks.

"Aunty! Let's say you gave Kamali and me some chores until this evening. And we agree and accept that as our responsibility. Suppose we want to play, then the responsibility to do the chore is limiting our freedom, right?"

"Well, you can ignore the chore and play all the time."

"How come, Aunty? I don't feel good about telling you one thing and doing another thing. You probably will be sad if we don't do the chores."

"Yes," Kamali joins. "I don't like to see you sad, ma."

Kavya and Uma adore the kids. They speak the truth. At this age, for most of the kids, the boundaries of what to do and not are determined by what emotions the parents or elders show them.

"Well, how do you feel about not doing the chore? Let's say the chore is cleaning all the utensils we use to cook and eat," chips in Uma.

"I don't feel good about not doing what I agreed," Kamali says. Neha nods in agreement.

"I understand, honey! Other than seeing me unhappy or sad, if you don't complete it, is there any other reason for doing the chore? What happens if we trusted that you both will do and come back to the kitchen just in time for dinner preparation?" Kavya has the girls thinking.

"Yes, dinner will be late."

"And…"

"You will have utensils to clean," Kamali speaks.

"But we can go and take care of it," Neha interjects.

"Even if you do, could it still be on time as planned earlier?" Kavya extends the question.

"We will be late for sure."

"Yes, when we don't do some things, other things will not happen on time. And sometimes that could bring difficulty to many of us. Delay in dinner is simple. We all are in good health, and no one will likely be affected. Let's say one of us has an ulcer, and they need to eat on time. In that case, their ulcer might get worse." Kavya gives a medical example.

"Hmm! You, our mothers, do so many things so that we can go to school on time, eat on time, and sleep on time. If you don't do what you do for us because you want to do whatever you may please, then we won't be able to do anything well," Kamali is thoughtful.

"Well said! Look at our bodies. If they wanted to do whatever they please, could we even survive? The lungs breathe nonstop, the heartbeats until it cannot, intestines work in a timely fashion, and whether it is our hands or our legs, they simply co-operate." Kavya shares.

"But our bodies are us, aren't they Ma?" Neha asks.

"Our body is a part of us. Just like a car has many parts, what we call 'I' has many parts. The physical body is the easiest to identify. There is mind, and there is something beyond the mind," Uma shares.

"What is that?" asks Neha.

"There is the life force, which is the source of the mind. If waves are the mind, then water is the life force. The life force is what makes the body work, I think."

"So, when I say my name is Neha, what am I saying?"

"The name Neha is similar to the address of this building. It helps to identify. What you say as Neha is a combination of life force, mind, and body."

"Then, everybody has these three. But we are not the same, isn't it?" Kamali asks.

Uma elaborates further, "We don't look the same way. We don't do things exactly the same way as each other. We don't all think exactly the same. This is because of how different our experiences are."

"I am confused, Aunty. The body changes as it ages. The mind is not an organ. The life force is not an organ. The mind can change. And I don't know how to locate the life force. So when I say I am Neha, what am I really saying?"

"Well, there is time and opportunities to learn more about it, honey! We are still learning," says Uma gently.

Kavya speaks. "Some people say the life force is the real self, 'I.' I don't know much about that. I think I'm the combination of all these three: the life force or self, mind, and body. This was shared by a lovely human being and a saint, Vethathiri Maharishi. For all practical purposes of living, I think this understanding helps."

"Okay. How are all these connected to liberty and responsibility?" asks Kamali.

"We can eat as much we can. It is our liberty. Beyond a limit, we better not eat. If we do, then there is a consequence. Bloated stomach, less energy sometimes you may vomit. Response + Ability is responsibility. How well I can respond to anything determines how response-able; responsible, we are," Kavya explains.

"The Body's liberty is made possible by its responsibility. The body can run, walk, write, speak, draw - all these are made possible by the responsibility undertaken of the life force, mind, and the body itself. Your body can do whatever, whenever, in realistic limits because it is healthy. Being healthy requires choosing and doing activities that promote health.

Eating and exercising well and developing the mind so that it does not give harmful instructions to the body are necessary for a healthy life. Such a healthy person can do more things and participate in many activities. All these actions are responses. While we are alive, there are always things we need to respond to. As silly as it may sound, we respond to food by eating, for example. We respond to the air by breathing. We respond to others' talks, activities, and even to what we conclude as their thoughts.

How well we respond determines how free we can be, and consequences are the boundaries of freedom. Understanding consequences help a free mind to be responsible and expand the boundaries. But we will always have boundaries. And our freedom is best enjoyed within the boundaries of consequences. For example, if I overeat, I get sick, and I cannot do as many things as I am when I am not ill. I hope I am making sense, kids," Uma lovingly looks at Neha and Kamali.

"Very clear, ma!"

"Yes, Aunty."

They both run and hug Uma and Kavya.

"Now, go play and enjoy the freedom," says Uma.

"Responsibly," giggles Kavya.

If there is someone who does not want us to be responsible,
who would they be?

12

A Bottle, its Label and Content!

Rachel is making toast for Surya and Krishtopher. Surya likes to eat his toast with Mango jelly. He meticulously applies the jelly and butter, almost with a master chef's skilled precision. Krish is liberal with the jelly. He sandwiches the slices of toast together, causing the jelly to escape out the edges with each bite. Surya fondly smiles at his son. Krish expects a question from Surya but is only met with silence.

Rachel joins them and spreads peanut butter and jelly on her slices. Ever since she went to the United States on an assignment, she has become a PB&J fan.

"Surya! This is not a science experiment. You could add some more jelly."

"I could, honey! And someday I will, but not today." Surya continues his meticulous application of the jelly.

"Dad! Take a bite from my sandwich. And tell me how it is. I bet after you do, you will ask me to put the jelly on your bread from now on." Krish extends his sandwich. Surya happily takes a bite.

"It sure is tasty, Krish! I would like to eat as you do, maybe at dinner, after which I could sleep. If I do what you do now, I will sleep instantly. Sugar gets me."

"Come on, Dad! You are exaggerating!"

"No Krish, really. By the way, I want to digress a bit and talk about something else. Is that okay?"

"Uh, oh! What now? Okay, go ahead, dad."

Rachel laughs at Krish's expression and nods to Surya in agreement.

"You know something, guys! Even the worst sandwich is better than just looking at a beautiful photo or recipe about the world's best sandwich, especially when you're hungry. I read this in a book, and how true it is, isn't it?"

"Yes. What are you getting at, honey?" Rachel asks.

"We have heard the saying, 'a map is not the territory'. People can immediately see the truth through these examples because they're not personal. But when it comes to the words we speak, we behave as if the map is the territory.

Take it a step further. A religious person who is emotionally involved in their specific faith claims their symbol is better than the others. The symbol represents a common truth that is shared by other symbols from other religions. But people who are emotionally drenched in their symbols do not shake off their feelings and see the truth represented by the symbol.

I find most religions keep truth and love as the basis of their symbols and a representation of God. Yet, current followers fight over which God is better, defeating what they consider God.

This, unfortunately, has extended to science as well. When scientists fight for their conclusions as if they are final and fixed, they reject other possibilities: truth itself.

What I say is right, and what others say is wrong. I find this more and more common as I study about mind and share what I discover."

"Hmm, yes. This is a problem as old as humanity, I think," Rachel agrees.

"But Dad! I look at this glass bottle with Mango jelly. It has different content compared to another with strawberry jelly.

Just like you, I prefer Mango jelly, too. And Mom likes Strawberry jelly better. Aren't the two bottles different?"

"Yes. At the same time, they both represent jelly. The fundamental use or nature of jelly is the same, while the flavors are different. The question really is if we can accept others choosing a different flavor than what I like. Should I fight with them the Mango jelly is better, and in fact, it is the only real jelly, and others are fake?"

"It is absurd to fight over the jelly," says Krish.

"I agree. Now, suppose if no one likes Mango jelly except you, you learn that it will not be produced anymore. How do you feel?"

"Hmm, that's bothering! But it is unrealistic."

"So are our fears! But if we fear this, then we will want to make sure everyone prefers Mango jelly."

"Why would we fear it?"

"Because you think all your happiness comes from the Mango jelly! Or at least of all the things that you like, Mango jelly provides the most happiness. Now, replace the Mango jelly with an attractive girl, or a handsome man, or a beautiful piece of land, or a magnificent riverside, or a country with appealing features, or anything you like! Your likes determine the quality of your and others' lives until you stop making a big deal of those likes and dislikes.

The same goes for things that you think you need; an idea that your God protects you always, or an idea that you need your friends to be available for you, etc. Your belief about what you think you need is enough to start a war. That's what has created all the wars to date."

"It is true," Rachel agrees.

Krish asks, "How can we remove this fear?"

"First, note we don't need to remove fear entirely. Fear can also be healthy. Understanding the fear makes it go away or take action. For example, you have a month's supply of food. But you are panicking as if all the food you have will be gone tomorrow. Understanding facts helps remove fear."

"How can you understand the fact about God? Isn't it left to a person's experience?" Rachel asks.

"Absolutely! At the same time, the principle behind God, as spoken and written in most religions, is truth and love. There is a commonality."

"Mom! Dad! You are losing me. I don't understand what you are talking about." Krish says.

"Let me explain this way, Krish. By now, scientists and psychologists agree that everything - action, thought, and emotion - are all choices. Although thought and emotion are not in our control unless we train the mind. Do you ever have thoughts flying all about, and you don't know how they started? Or have you ever had emotions that you didn't understand how they started dancing through your body?"

"Yes."

"For someone like you or I, it is still a theory that we can choose a thought or an emotion, at will, and at any time. People who trained their minds for years are able to achieve this. The world is full of ordinary people, let's say 95%. And when that 95% don't have control over their thoughts and emotions, what happens? We cling to what we think gives us desirable feelings and emotions. We want more of those things to prevail and less of the negative. We want certainty and predictability about everlasting comfort and pleasure."

"Now I'm getting it."

"Next, imagine everyone thinks that way, and what everyone thinks they want for their happiness is different from what everyone else wants. Undisciplined and uncontrolled minds often create fights, violence, and war. Historically, people are not able to break free from those tendencies. A small percentage of men and women have evolved beyond those habits, but not enough to stop others from wrecking the planet and the lives of everyone else.

Consider for a moment we are living through a pandemic; we are taking so many actions to control this 'disease.' I read somewhere that the deaths due to air pollution in India are five times greater than that caused by the pandemic. I think it could at least be two times in case if the news report is exaggerated. Yet, air pollution goes unchecked and untouched by plans and actions that don't have any lasting effect. Why?"

Krish is getting what his father is passionately communicating to him. "Because we want the industries that make things for us to keep producing them, and we want the vehicles which deliver the products to us to continue doing so?"

"Unfortunately, yes, you are right!"

Krish asks, "So what is needed for us to stop the cycle?"

Surya says, "An undying motivation, a pure desire to be alive, fresh and engage with life. At least that's what it is to me, and I must thank all my teachers - the thinkers who dared to walk the path. Our senses of taste, touch, smell, sound, and vision are lovely.

We can either employ our senses to constantly chase pleasure or use them as navigation and motivation to experience what life offers. As we engage with life, we experience a different kind of pleasure. In this case, pleasure does not become the goal we seek. Instead, it remains a welcome side effect, a positive consequence of our commitment to live life fully."

"Is this why many people starve, fast, and train their body?" Rachel asks.

"That may be their objective. Only a few are able to do those practices and not lose sight of the goal. The mere punishment of one's body does not get them anywhere, I feel. Many honest and great thinkers I know have spoken against such practices. I also think in our attempts to tame our body through forced deprivation, we spoil our sensitivity and love."

"Dad! I am not able to understand what you're saying!" Krish earnestly admits.

"See here, my dear Krish! Overuse of our senses wanting or craving more and more pleasure results in only experiencing physical and emotional gratification. The subtler things in our body, such as the mind itself and the life force behind it, are forgotten. Experience of the subtler aspects brings freshness in the body that is very different and much better than what we can feel through the stimulation of our senses. Our entire society is built on stimulation these days. For example, almost anywhere you go, there are small convenience stores where you can buy candy, among other things.

Here we use our sense of taste to experience happiness only when our sense of taste is stimulated. The more and more we condition ourselves to engage this simple gratification, the more we become addicts to its pleasurable sensations and the associated emotions we experience.

Our minds attempt to experience the entire world and its beauty with the only tool we came with, our body. There is a life force or self that runs everything, and our minds are capable of being in touch with that force by reducing its activity.

When I say 'I' or 'We,' I refer to the person as one unit—the unit comprised of body, mind, and life force.

In this whole unit, when the mind experiences the life force, all fears and frustrating attempts to find pleasure will cease. It is as if all the waves go back to the center of the sea and merge. At this moment, there is an opportunity for a new way of life and aliveness that we have not yet experienced. I want that. I had glimpses of that. And perhaps this is what religious and spiritual people refer to as enlightenment. I don't know.

But I do think for humanity to survive, this experience is very much needed. Having tasted this nectar, our minds will not go after stimulating the body to feel pleasure as an addiction. I think we require a free mind that is guiltless, simple, and honest to create this freshness."

"Thank you, Dad! Would you include me in your morning meditations? I want to meditate with you".

"By all means." Surya smiles.

Rachel holds Surya's hands tight and looks lovingly into his honest and calm eyes. Krish enjoys this sight of his parents and quietly takes a photo of them.

What makes something real?

13

Lost Child!

Neha and Kamali come running to Clark. "We planted a mango seed! We did! Oh Yeah! We did!"

Clark enjoys their celebration. "Well done, kids! Just one?"

Kamali says, "No! We did ten actually. And at the location you suggested, Uncle Clark!"

"Good! Come, let's go home! Kavya is waiting for us to eat."

"Okay!" The kids are excited and run towards home. Clark smiles and walks behind them.

"Mom! What did you make today?" Neha does not wait for the answer. She opens all the lids and finds Kavya has made curry with jackfruit seeds, dhal, and mushroom fry. She is excited about all the dishes; they are her favorite ones. Kamali likes the jackfruit seeds curry very much.

"If you eat those seeds, will a tree grow in your little tummies?" Kavya enters the kitchen with a smile.

"Ooh! That will be too much to handle, Aunty."

"I wouldn't have believed a seed could grow into a tree if I had not experienced it firsthand," says Clark, entering the kitchen too.

"When was your first experience, Dad?"

"When I was growing up on our family ranch. My father used to take me every day to plant something or another. It was fascinating for me how huge plants and trees grew out of little seeds.

One day, I cut open a seed to find what was inside. I thought there must be something. I found nothing. I went to my father and asked how the small seeds became large trees." Clark pauses.

"And what did he say? What did he say?" Neha jumps.

"He said that he didn't know and asked me to go to the town library to find any books I could on the subject. I did. I went every day and read numerous science books and journals. I learned quite a bit, and yet I didn't find the answer I was looking for. Science explains how things work, but it cannot yet explain the source."

"I don't understand, Uncle. What do you mean?" Kamali asks.

"Kamali, in your science book, does it explain how digestion works, for example?"

"Yes, Uncle. We are very clear about how the intestines work, what happens to the food, etc."

"Good, and what makes the organs work? How do they know what to do?"

"The mind tells the organs."

"I am not sure if that is true. Let's say it is! What makes the mind work? What is the source of the mind?"

"Hmm, I don't know." Kamali is pondering.

"I don't know for sure either. Over the years, I developed an idea. I derived this idea while inspired by many deep thinkers, meditators, and people who dedicated their lives to studying mind, body, and self. When the mysterious life force within us leaves, the body and mind cease to exist. Perhaps this is what makes everything work. This is what even gives the mind intelligence."

"How do we know for ourselves?" Neha asks.

"By training the body and the mind," Clark answers.

"Did you experience the life force consciously, Dad?"

"I have come in touch with it, honey, from time to time."

"Can you teach us, Uncle?" Kamali asks.

"Your father is an expert at it, Kamali! I learned from him. I'm happy to talk to him, and we will train you."

"Me too, please!" exclaims Neha.

"Come, let's eat." Kavya leads everyone to dine.

They all sit on the floor with legs folded. Kavya serves everyone the food, enclosed in banana leaves.

After lunch, all four go to the coconut fields to rest for a while.

"Dad! I see someone at the house by the door. A boy!"

"Yes. I'll go check." Clark walks to the house. "I will join you," Kamali walks along.

The boy is four or five years old. He looks frightened. Clark asks Kamali to talk to him. Clark thinks that the boy might get more scared if he speaks to him.

"Hi! How are you? How may we help you?" Kamali asks in a gentle voice and holds the boy's hands. The boy feels a bit comforted and opens his lips.

"I, I want Mom."

Kamali realizes that the boy is lost. Clark gets it too.

"We will find your Mom. Come inside and we will have some food while my uncle finds your Mom."

Kamali takes the boy inside, helps him wash his face and feeds him. Kavya and Neha also come back home.

After the boy finishes eating, Kamali asks him, "What's your name? What is your Mom's name?"

"Mohan. My Mom, my Mom, my Mom's name is Ma!"

He is so cute; they all understand that he doesn't know his Mom's name.

"Do you have something in your pocket? Could you give it to me?" Kamali asks.

The boy hands the things from both his pockets to Kamali. One thing is a tiny pack of candies, the other things are a pack of groundnut chikki - peanut brittle - in a wrapper, and a small whistle.

Clark takes the peanut brittle and sees that it's a local product, that is, a store's own, and he sees the name and address of the store printed on the wrapper.

"Okay, we have a good lead. Let's go to the store with the boy."

Everyone gets in the car with a sense of urgency, while remaining calm. Kamali speaks words of assurance to the boy. The store is in a nearby town, which is just five kilometers away. Clark thinks that the boy's parents must be in the town or in a neighboring village.

They have just driven a kilometer. Kavya asks Clark to stop. Clark pulls over by the sandy road.

"Look in the field, Clark. It seems they are searching for something. Maybe they are looking for the boy."

She points to all the people in the field looking around for something, some frenetically and some others methodically. The field was close to the road, and Kavya was instinctively looking at the road's side by which their own farm and fields are located. She had a hunch they could find some people looking for the kid.

Kavya asks the others to wait in the car and walks to the people. She takes the things from the boy with her in her handbag.

When she reaches them, she asks a woman who is almost her age what they are looking for. The woman might have cried for a long time. Her eyes are red, and the pain in her face is evident.

"My nephew! A little boy, four years old. His mom and dad were visiting us. I was going to the Siva temple in Nallur, and he was adamant that he would also go with me. I finally agreed and brought him. My husband was coming on another scooter. When we returned from the temple, we stopped for my husband Ram to go to the restroom.

My nephew ran after my husband but quickly strayed somewhere. We thought maybe my little darling started playing hide and seek, his favorite game, and hid somewhere we couldn't find him." She was sobbing as she spoke.

Kavya asked if they got the boy a snack or something. Without thinking about why she would ask that question, the woman answered, 'Yes! We got his favorite chikki from our own store. We always keep a big pile of it in our home whenever he visits," and starts crying aloud.

Kavya hugs her then tells her the boy is with them. The woman, Rama, is so happy and immediately asks where Mohan is. When Kavya points to their car, Rama does not wait for Kavya and runs to it, followed by the other searchers who were listening to the conversation.

As soon as Rama nears the car, the boy leaps on to her with a big smile. Rama kisses him on both cheeks nonstop, alternating from side to side. Kavya catches up and is delighted to see the boy and Rama together.

"He is my nephew, and I feel him as my son, sister!" Rama folds her hands in Namaste and deep gratitude to Kavya.

Kavya's eyes are tearful too. She knows the pain of a mom. She holds Rama's hands and comforts her, saying that Rama and her search party would have found the boy anyway. She then introduces Kamali to Rama, saying it was she who spotted the boy first.

Rama hugs Kamali and keeps thanking her. By now, she and the other searchers are relaxed and feel relieved. Kavya and Kamali introduce themselves and their family to Rama and all the others, and they all exchange greetings.

Clark suggests Rama and her husband should always keep their address and phone number with kids in a way that they won't lose it. Stick it to a toy they would never part with and also keep it in their pockets, or maybe pin it on something that it is not easily lost.

"I am so relieved, sister. I was worried he had been taken by the kind of people who put kids to begging as a business. Really! I would have died if he was not found."

"Relax, Rama. India still has a lot of goodness left in her people. Such things won't happen. Here, please eat this. Otherwise, you won't have the energy to carry the boy." Kavya gives her an apple. She always has fresh fruits stocked in the car every morning, in a temperature-proof container.

Rama graciously accepts the apple. Clark is talking to Rama's husband, Ram. Kamali and Neha engage the little, sweet Mohan. He is carefree, relaxed, and happy to have met Kamali and Neha. He giggles a lot.

Rama and Ram invite Kavya and family to their home. Kavya accepts and promises to come next week and meet the rest of the family.

Ram gives his phone number and asks Clark to get anything from the store anytime for free. Clark respects Ram's sentiment, thanks him and accepts the offer, but only for the first visit.

Kavya, Clark, Neha, and Kamali return to the farm. Kamali and Neha are lost in contemplation. Clark and Kavya let them be, undisturbed.

Once they arrive at the farm, Clark goes to water the trees. Kavya gets ready for the 4 p.m. visit to her clinic. She usually returns by 6:30 these days, unless someone needs assistance. Neha and Kamali hold hands and go for a walk.

It is 7 p.m. when Naren and Uma arrive. They confirm that they can move into Kavya's parents' home, which is a source of great joy for both families, especially for the kids.

After dinner, they all go stargazing. After a while Neha ask, "Is it true there are people who would kidnap kids and put them to begging, mom?"

Kavya and Clark realize what Neha and Kamali were contemplating earlier.

"I want to say no. But it's true, dear. Some people are lost in life. They don't have love in their hearts, so can do such things," Kavya says painfully and gently. She looks into her daughter's eyes and sees fear and agony.

Neha starts sobbing. She attempts to speak but loses her words. Kamali shares the feelings of sorrow and fear, goes to her friend and holds her hands.

The parents give their kids space and time. Kamali speaks softly, "I am also shocked, Neha. I read some news a few months ago in a local newspaper about such an incident and did not want to believe it."

"We say India is great. It is the home of spirituality. Then why, Dad? Why do such things happen?"

Clark embraces Neha. "Such things happen all over the world, my child. Different crimes against all people; children, women, and men, occur in almost every country. Some people lose their way of creating a healthy and peaceful life. We all begin life as babies.

Happy and joyful babies. As some grow up, due to various factors, they become cold-hearted, and make what they need and want so important beyond any expense with no regard to anyone else."

"What does it mean, Dad? We can't stop such bad things at all?"

"We do our best, honey. But sometimes, it is not enough."

"So, all the kids need to be constantly afraid that something like this can happen at any time?" Neha is angry.

"Why, dear? Getting afraid imagining such a thing would happen is not necessary. It doesn't happen all the time and to all the kids. Understanding that such things happen and taking action are enough."

"What action can we take? We are small."

"Small is okay.

The actions would be enough, dear, to save us from potential danger. I will teach you what I know and will also take you both to a specialist."

Neha feels a bit better.

Clark and Naren go for a walk. They don't say anything to each other. Their minds are focused on the issue that Neha raised. Uma and Kavya sit with Neha and Kamali at the portico of the farmhouse.

Uma says, "I read in a report that 96,000 children are abducted every year, in India, and less than 25% are traced."

Kavya answers, "That is an official number. I think it could be far greater. I am not sure how they measure, but I read, perhaps in the same report, that 460,000 children are missing in the United States, and about 48,000 in Canada."

"I think that it might be different. When children are missing and are not traceable in India, they are most likely trafficked, or put into begging or - no, I don't want to say it. It breaks my heart."

"It breaks my heart too! The sad truth is that it happens to poor families where the parents are not equipped to thoroughly educate or inform their children. People like us can save our kids, educate and teach them, and look after them well. In poor families, the kids are on their own, whether they go to school or work. And such easy accessibility of the kids to antisocial elements is a concern."

"Yes, and law enforcement is not strong enough to make a significant dent in the problem."

"The only way is proactive education to kids and their parents about personal safety and protection. And more than that, to cull out abusive tendencies in people through education, reform, and rehabilitation."

Clark and Naren return. Naren tells Kavya and Uma that they have thought of actions concerning the issue on which they've been preoccupied. They want to work with the collector, the highest officer in administration in their district on an awareness camp. They also want to run an awareness campaign in Naren's YouTube channel and tour the district's colleges to garner support in the student community to spread the 'word and practices' to villagers and poor families living in city slums.

Kavya and Uma think that will be a very good start.

How do we bring lasting awareness to others?

14

Action

In the call with their friends and families, Clark is narrating the story of finding Mohan, while Naren interleaves and shares his thoughts on the actions they both considered. Natalia and Antonio, Ileana and Victor, Deborah and Pat, Rachel and Surya, Kathy and Will Rodgers are all in the call. Uma and Kavya also are present. It's a meaningful reunion.

"Are you guys going to start a movement or something? Perhaps a team or an organization?" Kathy asks.

"No. We would never do that. In our experience, that is the surest way of alienating ourselves from the rest of society. We want to garner support and get people talking about the issue of missing children and taking actions in their communities. But we definitely would not create another charity or organization. We have hundreds of them already.

People who are engaged in their jobs and earn their daily-living hand over the responsibility of education and protection to the hands of such organizers, the most prominent one being the government. One more team or organization will not suffice. We already have a large human team on this planet. Gradually, as common folks like us begin to speak about important things, others will come around. When people begin to educate themselves and participate in decisions that affect them and their communities, it will be just enough," Clark speaks.

"In those we are able to reach, there may not be many people taking such initiative. It's up to their own conscience. Our job is to plant the seeds just as a farmer. The farmer does not calculate which seeds will come to life and which will not." Naren adds.

"I agree." Pat nods.

"Educating boys and girls at an early age is necessary. It's not enough to just cram them with numbers and facts to memorize but to help them understand pain, pleasure, human motivation, joy, mind, and self.

When we understand these things from an early age, we need not depend so much on physical pleasure and positive emotions for happiness. We won't think feeling comfort and pleasure alone are the highest aspirations of human life. We would live differently.

In fact, there will be a different breed of humanity. It's a long-term goal, of course, but it's necessary to plant these seeds with a sense of urgency, as if it is now or never," Rachel chips in.

"Anything can be found on the internet. Almost any examination up to college can be cracked by running a search on google. Memory and memorizing will have little value in the future," Deborah weighs in.

Antonio speaks. "Mexico is in a similar state as in India, I think. As you all know, I'm a TV anchor, and I will do my best to convince our channel to have a permanent slot for awareness and education on the issue of the misuse and abuse of children."

It's Victor's turn. "I'm a film producer, and I commit funds every year for media - educational but interesting videos - short films and movies on the subject. I've been meaning to set aside some money for a social objective. I thought of making a film about traffic rules which could help prevent accidents. But now I think this issue is much more important."

Uma reads a report from the Human Rights Commission.

It is the statistics of missing children globally every year, including potential and actual causes. The numbers are shocking and startling.

They all hear the news with heavy hearts and firm resolution.

"I was unwilling to give up Indian citizenship and hence delayed applying for American citizenship for a while. Eventually, I did. When I became a US citizen, I was in tears. The judge who led the event honestly and passionately explained what made America the country it is. He made a very compelling call for participation in the community. And in that instant, I understood what a privilege it was to have been born in India and what India has offered me.

For a long time, I took for granted what India did for my life. Because I was born into citizenship, I did not value it. Becoming a US citizen reminded me of the value of India too. I told myself that I would do what I can, in my capacity, to both countries and to the rest of the world when I heard the judge speak. And I stopped diminishing my actions that they are small or short range. I must do what I can do." Uma speaks her mind.

"I am glad to know this about you, Uma!" Kathy is happy.

"As you all know, we live in an active community where people care about each other's lives. I'll share the news in our town hall meeting and engage willing people who can put time towards this awareness initiative," says Will.

"We just need to be clear on the point when anyone who participates wants to make an organization or a team with a name, that we don't support it," Clark says firmly.

"That is the most important thing you said, guys," says Ileana. "Many problems originate because we always get excited about making an organization, and eventually lose our focus and connection with the causes we support.

The organization, and who we are because we belong to it, gains more importance. We need everyone, and we don't need anyone who wants to alienate themselves as a crusader or a leader. A lot of harm is done with such self-righteous idealists."

"What we do, this initiative is part of our life, no less important than any of our other responsibilities. When we engage with such a spirit, it is easy to stay on the activities of each of the objectives," Kathy adds.

"There is a movie from 2016 you all might like to watch, *'Lion'*. It's directed by Garth Davis. A beautiful tale of a missing boy." Kavya shares, and after which the friends conclude the call.

Is there anything other than consistent action towards a cause that can bring lasting awareness about the cause?

15

'...isms!'

Neha, Kamali, Krishtopher, and Liam are in a video conference call. Liam, Kristopher's neighbor, is the son of Hannah and Elias, who are originally from Austria. Hannah and Elias moved to Australia two decades ago on a job, after which they decided to settle there and build their family.

From the time Kamali was born, Naren always wanted to have her study in a school founded by a like-minded friend that values humanity, systems, and ecological thinking.

One after the other, Naren's friends and Uma's friends followed suit. Thus, Neha, Krishtopher, and Liam are also in such schools.

Naren wanted Kamali to evolve from seeing the world and its parts, which often sees humans as objects, to viewing everything as relationships relative to her. At the same time, being a goal-oriented man, he also wanted Kamali to be equally focused on the destination as on the journey.

Kamali loves her school. When Naren noticed how excited she was to get to school in the mornings, he was delighted. In his childhood days, Naren studied in a school where teachers, the principal, and parents alike had one mission - get the students to score the highest grades at any cost, including physically beating them brutally.

Naren resisted the system but did not have many choices being a child of poor parents who did not know any better. He vowed to himself that he would give the best education to his children. Naren also supplements Kamali's schoolwork with the essential skill set he gained from traditional schools, such as memorizing and sitting through and completing long classwork notes.

He became more balanced in his view of the need to merge both worlds - a world of creative thinking and a world of physical effort.

At first, Kamali and her friends thought systems and ecological thinking were taught and practiced in only their schools. Thanks to the internet and a little research effort on their part, however, they learned that many people in the world practice such thinking. In fact, they soon discovered some of our visionary ancestors adopted such thinking practices centuries ago.

Last week, the kids made an important discovery. They were talking to each other about their experiences with a dog. It was startling for Kamali that Liam feels so repulsive about any dog. She could not comprehend why someone would not like a dog. She loves all dogs, whether they are the dirty and ugly ones from the street or well-fed and loved ones from the west.

The next day, having spent the previous day being upset about Liam's reaction to dogs, Kamali and the rest of the kids learned that he had been bitten on his face by a neighbor's dog when he was four years old. Little Liam was terrified and had to be taken to an emergency room right away.

The whole experience was traumatic for him, from when the dog attacked to getting the medical treatment and healing. Until then, the dog, who was a lovable buddy, became an enemy to little Liam.

Since that incident, Liam explained how his recall of the dog pouncing on him, his shock and emotions - fear, notably, were projected on each dog he saw in person or in a photo. His reaction to the memory further strengthened the emotions about the incident, and thus his aversion compounded.

Underneath his intense avoidance is a deep fear that he or a loved one who is with him will get hurt. Even though he has not been hurt by another dog after his unfortunate incident, he finds it challenging to be with any dog.

Kamali spent a week thinking about Liam, considering how she might have felt and reacted in the same situation, then believed she better understood him. Kamali, Krish, and Neha became more kind to Liam and started looking for ways to help him surpass the strength of his emotional aversion and fear of dogs. This led to a key discovery for the kids. When considered along with feelings, they figured out that human thinking is naturally systemic and not just thought-based logic.

They started listing different things, animate and inanimate, including people - their mothers, fathers, uncles, aunts, grandfathers, grandmothers, and siblings. After writing them out, the kids shared their experiences and emotions they built from all the interactions and how each experience shaped a previous one as the previous one influenced the present.

For example, Kamali had a previous experience with a lovable dog, then she came across a different dog that performed an adorable prank. Her experience with the first dog attracted her to the 'prankster' dog.

The dog's pranks improved her excitement about the dog she saw in the past and, in general, all dogs. Past memory influences the present experience, and the present experience also enriches the past memory.

Naren was overjoyed learning about the kids' lovely exercise. Surya gave the kids questions to think about.

"Is there any time other than the present that is real? Aren't the past and the future simply based on memories and imagination?"

The kids gleefully started journeying with the question. They still do.

Through experience and exploration, they understand ecological thinking focuses on relationships between everything and everyone. They know to differentiate cause and effect in relation to time and learn to estimate the consequences of a single action on many different elements.

Yesterday they did an exercise on what the effects of eating a sandwich at a restaurant could be - both positive and negative on the restaurant, their families, grocers, farmers, and their present and future health.

Now they are talking about different types of ideologies. Liam and Krish have an assignment from their school to understand capitalism, socialism, and communism.

Liam and Krishtopher talked about the assignment with Neha and Kamali two days earlier. Neha and Kamali became very interested and wanted to do the exercise too. All four did a bit of homework and research about these ideologies from different sources on the internet and have come together now to discuss what they learned. Naren and Clark ardently observe Neha and Kamali from a distance. An hour passes by quickly.

Kamali runs to Uma and Kavya to have them join the call. On the other side, Rachel and Hannah are joining Liam and Krish. It is the mothers with their children.

After exchanging greetings, Rachel asks one of them to summarize their understanding of the ideologies. Liam explains them very well.

Rachel asks, "So, what do you all think? Which system do you favor?"

Neha says, "Aunty! All three systems sound good. But as we researched the school of thought within each system, we often found destruction to people and the environment. In capitalistic societies, not all business owners care about the people involved in the production or about which countries they support. They don't care about the impact on the environment in those countries as much as their own.

In communistic societies, people eventually lose interest in creating anything and run away or perish.

In socialistic societies, there is chaos and indecisiveness, affecting the lives of all."

"I agree with Neha," says Kamali.

Liam says, "The issue is in how people implemented these ideologies. In my view, the origin of each ideology has got to do with a type of resistance to oppression."

Kavya is interested in hearing Liam. "That sounds thoughtful, Liam. Could you explain more?"

"Sure. In ancient times, I'm talking about the time of Christ, people who were traders and money lenders might have been ruthless in treating others who exchanged or borrowed from them. Christ fought that oppression. But what actually followed after his life was tragic. Trade and money were considered sinful by people in power. Perhaps, by denouncing traders, some religious people and autocrats who accumulated power and money gave birth to capitalism as a resistance. Either as resistance to oppression by autocrats or to selfish production, or a combination of both, communism and socialism were born. They condemned bad treatment of people, the environment, and needless production that depleted resources.

There are moral and sensible capitalists, communists, and socialists. But I believe such people are outnumbered by people without morals in each school of thought. And so is the nature of the business, politics, and everything else. Each of these venues reflects the quality of people."

"Wow, Liam! Thank you! That's such a good summary," Kavya exclaims.

"It may not be an accurate representation of what happened in history, but I believe it's a good, insightful imagination into how each school of thought was created," Rachel adds.

"So, given the limitations of today, which society would you rather be part of?" Hannah asks Liam.

"I would prefer capitalism." Liam answers without any hesitation. "Because the human spirit of freedom prevails better in this society than in the others."

"Yes, but at what cost?" asks Krish. "Look at how the people who are producing all our smartphones in China, India, and other countries live. What is the condition of their work environment? All over the world, the wealthy unknowingly subjugate the poor to trade their lives for a job to create pleasure and comfort for a small set of the population, over and over again."

Kamali says, "None of these systems in their current implementation are sustainable. They will perish. Unless they are corrupt, poor people will stay poor, not healthy, and struggle in all three systems."

"What system would you rather be part of?" Rachel asks Kamali.

Kamali says, "None of them."

"Is that an option in today's world?" Rachel asks, leaving Kamali to ponder.

"Which country would you like to go to for higher studies, other than India?" Uma asks Kamali lovingly.

"The United States, Australia, or New Zealand." Kamali answers.

Neha says, "I love to stay in India, with all its limitations. I think India will give birth to a new type of civilization."

Krish says, "I like your faith Neha. I'm also certain we all have a lot of work to do to sustain this earth for us to live."

Liam says, "I think India and the US are key to positive changes in the world. One country, a home of culture, and the other of technological innovation."

"On behalf of all my generation, I am sorry, kids. We brought this trouble to you. We were born in the way of life where everyone went after material wealth at the expense of many others in the world. The system hasn't changed yet, and although we are now aware, we still can't help being a part of it. We are doing our best to bring awareness to our generation and to all of you. Our efforts so far are modest in scope and limited to a few people, friends, and family!" Kavya is deeply apologetic.

"Mom! Is it not possible to change this trend?" Neha asks.

Kavya answers. "Only when a majority of people change, if not all. At the same time, I have hope that if we live an honest, loving, and straightforward life, we can create that small world for ourselves and those around us.

I went to Indonesia many years ago, where I witnessed a volcano that erupted a week earlier. For about two or three kilometers from the mouth of the volcano, everything was ashes.

What fascinated me was at about a half kilometer from the volcano's mouth, there was an unaffected strip of green.

The strip was almost in a circular form, and it was so lush and fresh. It was an unbelievable sight. Everything around and beyond the strip was ashes. How could have that happened? No one could tell. I believe that it was an act of compassion by Mother Nature. She left some green for generations to come.

I don't know if it's true or not. I mean, whether it is a fact. But my belief helps me keep going with a faith that at least a small group of sensible people will prevail even if the majority of us do not. That set of people will grow humanity with a new understanding and will make our future generations flourish.

And I don't know how to be part of that small group of people who survive if this were true. Nature has its own ways beyond our calculations. Even if we perish, how we die and what we have done until that time matters."

The kids look calm and peaceful. The adults are hopeful about how the kids will grow up - sensible, sensitive, and loving.

How do we deal with people who refuse to listen?

16

Narcissus!

Alexa is reading about Narcissism on Wikipedia. She already ordered a few books on the subject, which are highly rated by credible sources. Ever since Ileana mentioned Narcissism, she can't stop thinking about it. How does it occur in a child? Why? How can one, whether they are a child or an adult, get out of it? What would happen if they didn't? Her mind is churning with these questions all the time.

She is meeting Ileana and Amber for the evening. Ileana will pick Alexa up, after which all three are going to a movie followed by dinner. Alexa is writing questions in her iPhone 'Notes' application to ask Ileana. Meanwhile, Natalia and Antonio are getting ready for a date night. This is the first time they are going out after Natalia gave birth to Solange. Natalia's mother is taking care of Solange for the evening.

Natalia asks if Alexa needs anything. Alexa says there is nothing and asks if Natalia wants her to stay at home with grandma and be with Solange. Natalia is delighted at her daughter's care but mentions that it is not needed. Alexa checks with grandma also if she needs company. After ensuring that everything is taken care of, Alexa confirms with Ileana that the plan is still on.

Since she was born, Alexa has been surrounded by people, adults, and kids alike. She developed caring for people around her after various experiences and learnings where the creed of self-absorption just did not stick to her.

Alexa's combined family experience, friends and other family visiting her home without any appointments, and Natalia teaching her to look after neighbor's kids, helped develop Alexa into a caring person who is observant and active in helping others.

One of the themes of her journey as she's grown has been her experience with demanding children and adults who always wanted things their way. It surprises her that even some adults behave adamantly.

At this juncture, at Amber's house, she learned from Ileana the difference between grooming oneself, liking to buy things for oneself, and caring for oneself, versus feeling obsessed or absorbed with oneself.

There is a downside to the teachings to be unselfish, given by Alexa's family, too. It cost her unchecked expression as she started compromising her needs when giving in to kids and adults alike. She doesn't want to be labeled selfish and be cast out from any of her circles — her friends, study groups, or any of the school clubs.

"Thank you, Aunty," says Alexa as she gets in the car. Amber gives her a hug, and the jolly, good conversations begin right away. Alexa waits until they get to the ticket counter in the movie hall. As they walk from the counter with their tickets, Alexa asks Ileana, "Aunty! What does one lose because they are narcissistic?"

"Oh! I owe you one! We'll talk about it for sure. Why don't we walk to the food court and have our dinner before the movie starts? Amber, do you also want to join our conversation on this topic?"

"Yes, Mom, but not today. I want to walk around the mall a bit and check out a couple shops before the movie starts. Besides, I'm not at all hungry. May I pass? I will meet you both at the ticket counter."

"Very well, then," says Ileana.

"See you, Amber," says Alexa.

Ileana and Alexa hold hands and walk together.

Ileana speaks. "One loses many things if they are narcissistic. Tell me, what do you understand about the word?"

"One who has an inflated value of themselves is a narcissist."

"Can you explain that?"

Someone who is a narcissist wants attention only to themselves or more to themselves. They think only about what they want or need and not about others. Their Narcissism could be about how they look, their talent, or it may be simply about what they think of themselves."

"It seems you have been doing some research."

"Yeah, Aunty, I also relate what I studied with people I have encountered. I also listened to a Ted Talk where the presenter spoke about 'Grandiose Narcissism,' and 'Vulnerable Narcissism.'"

"Very good. What did you learn that was new to you?"

"To better oneself, one needs to accept their shortcomings. This is a simple but difficult path. As the narcissistic person's image is threatened if they accept their limitations, they will not choose this path. It is terrifying and sad."

"I understand that it's sad. Why is it terrifying?"

"Because they would not hesitate to hurt another person if they didn't get their way."

"That's a reasonable fear. There are hopefully only a few malignant narcissists. I mean, those who have ill will. Some people are harmless attention getters and not narcissists yet. If we don't do an honest assessment of our conduct and address the behavioral issues we find within us, without any guilt, we could end up confusing that we are a narcissist and/or incorrectly judge others who are not."

"Oh! Thank you so much for elaborating, Aunty!"

They eat quietly, and Ileana observes Alexa deep in thought and lets her be.

Ileana is thinking about the future of the world.

In the days where cinemas were the only entertainment besides TV, people looked at their ideological representations on the screen through the actors and actresses – the heroes and heroines.

Nowadays, anyone who has a mobile phone can start a YouTube channel and post something about themselves, maybe a song or dance, or a speech.

Everyone has been given the stage, the silver screen, and with maximum potential to reach a world audience, all with just the investment of your smartphone. Whether one would get a committed audience, fan base, or not, the opportunity exists.

What will be the long-term effect to movie actors and actresses?

When people are able to see themselves in a video, would this lessen their attachment to the traditional heroes and heroines?

It is not possible in most cases to replicate what their favorite heroes and heroines do as seen in films, as one cannot afford the cost of such a production.

Still, would opportunities to create personal YouTube channels at least bring down people's craze and help them be clear that what they are seeing on the screen is an imagined version of themselves?

Thus, they both are deep in thought. At the same time, Ileana is wary of petty thieves in the malls. She pays close attention to both their belongings but forgets to notice the time. Amber comes running to them.

"Mom! Alexa! What are you doing? Come on! The movie might have started already. I waited for you for a long while at the ticket counter."

"Oh! Sorry!" Both Ileana and Alexa apologize to Amber and run with her to the cinema hall. In a bit, they are all engaged in the beautiful and moving portrayal of the story of a little orphan child from India.

The movie **Lion** is in English, and the cinema complex owner has been playing meaningful films, old and new alike, at this period where people are mostly at home. He is an honest businessman and has taken good care of the facility, keeping it sterilized and making sure the staff are well educated and disciplined about the hygiene requirements during the pandemic.

They could not sit next to each other in the movie hall. The hall's capacity is 300, but only 30 are allowed these days, which places them safely apart.

The movie ends. It was a beautiful movie, and they walk with tearful eyes that shine in joy. Alexa speaks first. "Thank you, Aunty. It was a lovely movie, and it also answered a lingering question for me on how to recover a person from Narcissism."

"Oh, cool!" Ileana smiles.

"I think appealing to a person, just as a loving mom would do, in this movie, would be the best possible way. Give reassurance to the narcissistic person that you wouldn't think less of them if they were to admit their shortcomings."

"It's a good idea in theory and is probably a workable theory if we're talking with a person who also has a bit of awareness and cares about others. If it's someone who doesn't have a little of those characteristics, and who lied a lot to maintain their view of themselves, then they would suspect we're lying and it wouldn't work."

Amber understands what they might have talked about. She says, "Complex Humanity!"

"Yes, honey! I think that's what makes life on earth so valuable. We need to deal with our incredible intellect, a super-duper computer. I don't think any computer can match it. Maybe a computer can do certain things better, but as a whole, it's no match for the human mind.

Additionally, we need to deal with our bodies, which are dependent on others for survival and our emotions. In Indian philosophy, they say that one comes to the human plane to evolve, even if they are God. I understand why!"

"Why?" Alexa asks.

"Gosh! Look at our struggles in the world. And also look at the incredible achievements. We are still grappling with hunger issues for the entire world population, even though we produce one and a half times the amount of food required to feed everyone. This alone is a statement of our higher valued intellectual, discriminatory nature, which we hold in place to compensate for our underdeveloped compassion, love, and joy. We apply our intellect and various means to find more ways to achieve comfort and pleasure. Ultimately, our end goal is to buy joy and love. But we fail, as those values cannot be bought. They must be built through a change in perspective and willingness to exert effort to think and act."

"What perspective, Ma?" Amber asks.

"Be content with what we have and build things which consider all of us, not just our specific needs and desires. We get a lot of joy in return. It can take a person a long time to understand, but that doesn't matter. Such journeys make the human experience worthwhile."

"But if we take a long time, people are affected, poor people, and a lot. Isn't that true, Aunty?"

"Yes, materially and/or soulfully poor. However, there is no other way. Change is gradual and proportional to a person's desire to change."

"We are taught a desire is a bond that affects us, Aunty. Why do you say a desire of the person determines the change?"

"Desire as motivation is one thing. Desire as an addiction is another thing, which is ultimately against the movement of motivation. Desire is a powerful impulse that can be used to motivate us to evolve and help others. On the other hand, it can be used to chain ourselves in the dreamland about us, what is comfortable and pleasurable, and chase those while forgetting the cost to others."

"Got it, Aunty!" Alexa is happy.

Alexa continues. "Whether or not we can change a person who is deep into themselves, their image, their Narcissism is not a question. Could we develop an intellect that is motivated by a desire to help others? And with this motivation, can we become flexible to reach a person to help, but be wise to move away if they are destructive? This is the question, I think."

"Right on the money!" Ileana claps her hands.

"Aunty! That reminds me of another thing. How much do I need to pay you for the movie and dinner?" Alexa asks.

"It is on me, honey! Thank you for your company!"

"Thank You, Aunty. Next time it is on me. I'm saving money from my odd jobs."

"Deal." Ileana smiles and hugs Alexa. Amber joins them. They all soak in their care for each other.

Why is it difficult to change a habit?

17

Saint

Liam arrives at home after school. He looks a bit confused. Hannah notices immediately but doesn't ask anything. She doesn't like to intervene unless it's really necessary.

Liam asks Hannah how her day was. She tells him that she met a friend for lunch, which was nice, and that she has been writing all the rest of the day. Liam knows his mom is writing a book on Yoga.

His face brightens.

"Mom! I have a question on Yoga, but I want to find everything I can first and then ask you."

Hannah smiles.

"Shall we go for a walk at seven o'clock?"

"Yes, is dad joining us?"

"Likely, but I'm not sure."

Liam goes to the garden. He likes to lie down on the grass and read. As it is chilly, he prefers a chair and continues to read the book he brought from the school library. There is an outdoor lamp to use when the sunlight dies out. The book he's reading in an English translation of Yoga Sutras, which means formulas, of Patanjali.

Inside, Hannah is refining her write up for a chapter. She is an ardent practitioner of Yoga since childhood, thanks to her mother.

Hannah's mother taught her physical Yoga - yogasanas - when Hannah was seven. Yoga focuses on making the mind a clean mirror that reflects one's thoughts, actions, and the unknown presence called life or life force. Some call it soul; others call it spirit.

The physical exercises that one learns as part of Yoga prepare the body to be still, motionless in meditation, which renders many health benefits.

A well-trained Yogi can transmit their condition just as a radio station relays its sound waves to the tuned-in radios. The Guru that Hannah studied with was a man of such caliber. Being wary of the fake Gurus, Hannah's mother took quite some time to test the training she received and find the truth for herself. She was in awe at the efficacy of the system and became a dedicated and sincere practitioner. The system and the guide do not demand anything, and everyone is left to their own will and wish to practice.

As a result of years of dedicated practice in meditation and introspection, Hannah concluded that words and concepts are tools for understanding and communicating about reality. They are not reality itself, so Hannah will not engage in intellectual discourses or arguments with people who use different words and concepts.

Hannah never planned to write a book until her friends urged her. They worry about the distrust people develop upon experiencing false Gurus and fake self-help experts. They want to help people not feel discouraged by turning their unfortunate experiences into deterrents in finding Gurus and experts who genuinely serve humanity.

"It's sad," Hannah thinks. "These days, we need to qualify words with 'true,' and 'genuine' - 'true Guru,' 'truly serving humanity,' etc. If we didn't give in to temptations, lies, and ill-will, our lives would not have degraded so much."

She sighs.

Whenever she feels hopeless, she sits in meditation and prays to nature. The larger life that holds all life does not judge her worries and fears. She feels rejuvenated after such experiences.

Elias arrives home and walks into the living room with a huge dog. Hannah is delighted and surprised at the sight of the dog. Elias didn't say anything about bringing a dog home when he left in the morning.

"This is Saint. Saint was orphaned after Mrs. Madeline Kemp died last week. You might remember meeting the Kemps a couple of times at our office parties. I learned everything about our business from her husband, George Kemp. Especially after George passed away two years ago, Saint was everything to Madeline. She wrote a note to Olivia, the HR manager, to find a suitable and willing person in our office to take Saint home and care for him.

Olivia said Madeline always considered everyone in the office as her family when she spoke to us today. She asked if any one of us would be willing to take Saint. You and Liam told me last week I could choose a dog to bring home. So, I knew you wouldn't mind and I wanted to surprise you. I also didn't want anyone to choose Saint before me. After I offered, Olivia told me that Madeline had given a list of people she thought would take good care of Saint. However, she also entrusted Olivia to find the person.

Hannah kneels down and looks at the dog. Saint has kind eyes.

"He certainly qualifies to be called a Saint. I will hold you to cleaning after your dog, though." Hannah chuckles.

"Alright, alright!" Elias laughs.

Hannah loves dogs and has been wanting to bring a dog home for a few months now. Elias walks outside to Liam. Liam looks up, then closes the book immediately at the sight of Saint and runs to him. Thanks to his Kristopher and Kamali's persistent work, Liam lost the fear of dogs.

Elias tells Liam, "Meet beloved Saint, Liam."

They both sit next to Saint, and Hannah joins them. They are sitting on the grass, and it's not as chilly as they expected. The dog barks lovingly and gently.

"His eyes are incredible, Dad. He is so kind."

Elias tells his son, "Yes, he is. We're lucky that he's with us. They say his natural life span is thirteen years. I hope that Saint lives longer than that. He's already eleven."

Saint barks lovingly again and climbs on Liam. Liam fondly caresses Saint's head.

"Mom, shall we take him along with us on our walk?"

"Sure! Maybe he can share his views too, on your question," his mother playfully teases.

"Oh! I don't have any questions, ma. I have answers brewing in me as I read the book, and I will ask you at the end of the week if there are any questions."

"That's a quick change of heart. But it's all good. Let me change my clothes and join you."

Hannah and Elias both walk into the house while Liam continues to play with Saint.

The family enjoys the walk by the seashore. Unless they're out of town, they don't miss a day to walk on the beach. Elias and Hannah are walking at a slower pace than Liam and Saint. Elias reaches for Hannah's hand and asks, "How is your book coming along?"

"It's coming well. I attempt to describe Yoga in simple terms without any disrespect to authors and Gurus who spent almost all their lives in codifying Yoga. I'm also writing about how to identify a real Guru. My care to write well demands a lot of time. And I'm not sure if I'll make the deadline."

"Does it affect your publisher?"

"I asked them. The publisher said they're fine. They've known me for so long. I don't think they would tell me even if they are affected. Part of me wants to rush the work out of respect for them. But another part wants to refine the writing to bring a simple and quality product. I have no better choice other than to thank them for understanding and continue what I am doing."

"Knowing you, I think that's best in the long run." He smiles at her warmly and gently squeezes her hand.

Hannah asks, "How was Mrs. Madeline? You told me she was in her last moments and that we could go and see her."

"It's one of my regrets that we didn't go in time. I thought we would have been able to go this weekend."

"Yes, I remember you telling me."

"I heard she left her life quietly in her sleep. The maid found Madeline on her bed with an unmoving and radiant smile when she showed up for work in the morning.

The maid's name is Zaloo. I met her along with Saint this evening after I left the office. Saint is very fond of her.

Hannah! How do you feel about getting Zaloo to work with us for two or three days a week? It might help you focus on your book."

"I like that idea. If you're sure, you should call and ask for Zaloo's service before she is hired by someone else."

"Ha, ha! Sure, I will do it as soon as we get home."

They both watch Liam joyfully playing with Saint. The dog responds to his love and plays with him.

"Liam! Come back!" Elias calls aloud.

"Okay!" Liam answers aloud and turns to Saint, "Come on, buddy! Let's see who runs faster."

Saint doesn't outrun Liam. Liam thinks Saint likes to be together and doesn't want to run ahead of him.

"You know, if you reverse DOG, you get GOD. It's a funny and poignant thing told by a Guru", Hannah states.

Liam nods in agreement. "Yeah, I heard that as well. Gratitude and loyalty are essential to evolve ourselves. Who else but the DOG is an exemplary leader of these virtues?"

"A genuine teacher takes these virtues to death. There is a gulf of difference between discipline that is demanded and discipline that is naturally built through love. We listen to a physician and do not rebel, but we rebel with our teachers. When we understand that a true teacher wants nothing more than friendship and gives all of their time, we can become better students."

"That would be good."

Liam walks to Elias. "Thank you, Dad!"

"You bet! Come, let's go home."

Saint runs to Elias and walks along with him. Elias had visited George and Madeline when Saint was just a few months old. After then, he had visited them only a few times in the past decade. Elias wonders what makes Saint bond with him so well.

All three walk cheerfully back to the house, with their laughter adding to the energy of the evening sun.

A week passes by, and all three are watching a movie one evening. Liam used his own savings, bought all the components for a home theater a couple of months ago, and assembled it himself. He always works during the summer. He repairs cars, fixes ATVs, and computers since he was eight years old.

Thus, he is quite known in the neighborhood as the local resident fixer. Elias and Hannah asked him to save the money he earned and put it in his piggy bank.

When Liam wants anything new, he first spends the earnings in his bank before asking his parents.

The phone rings. Elias answers the call.

The call lasts just two minutes. Elias turns to Liam and Hannah and says, "Olivia wants to visit me and says it's about an important matter. Are you both okay with me asking her to come over?"

"Yes," they answered unanimously. Liam says they can always continue the movie after the visit.

Hannah knows Olivia from an office party, after which they became friends through a common interest; they are both movie buffs. They like to go to movies together, and also shopping from time to time.

Liam answers the door when Olivia arrives. As soon as they both enter the living room, Saint rushes to Elias's lap. Elias knows Saint is very affectionate, but he finds Saint's enthusiasm to be up a notch this time.

He asks Saint, "What's up, buddy?"

Olivia is overjoyed to see how well Saint feels at home in Elias, Hannah, and Adam's life.

Fifteen minutes become thirty, and then an hour. Olivia is actively speaking with all three of them. After an hour and a half, Olivia opens her briefcase and takes out a file.

"Okay, guys! Thanks for having me here. This is something for Elias, but I don't think he'll mind me reading it to all of you. I know I walked into your movie. Sorry. Is it okay?"

"It's fine, please go ahead," says Hannah.

"Dear Olivia,

I hope this finds you well. If you are reading this WILL, it means I am with you and Saint only in spirit. Saint's is no ordinary life. He uses all his time to express love. This is why he is extraordinary.

People may laugh that I say such things about a dog. But I know him. He didn't get his name from any random choice or decision.

Whenever I had a headache, Saint would reach to me and keep his paws on my head. My headache would disappear. Saint had done this with me more than a dozen times, and every single time it helped me recover.

George loved him. We took him as a puppy, not from a shop but from the street. A neighbor complained to the city corporation about a stray dog, which was Saint's mother. At those times, we knew what would happen when the dog-van entered our street. Dogs like Saint's mother, dirty and with skin disease, were never spared. Saint's mother had some lumps on her body too. The corporation used to kill such dogs as a preventive and safety measure against disease.

I noticed she was pregnant. But I didn't realize she was going to deliver so soon. She died right after giving birth to Saint, and in front of our doorstep. And there was this cute and innocent puppy! He was sitting by his mother quietly and was looking at her eyes.

The corporation people could only take the dead body of Saint's mother. I told them I would take care of Saint.

Saint watched her mother's body being taken away. I felt so sad and was not sure what he felt. He looked at me with such kindness and gratitude. At the same time, he has a majestic demeanor about him. To us, he is our son, right from that instant.

I want him to be loved and taken care of after I depart. I want someone in George's office to take him home. I made a list of people from your office who I respect and know to be loving souls. I request you present an open invitation to all the folks in the office.

I might have missed someone who is genuinely loving and caring if I stick to my list alone. Or the people on that list might not be able to take care of Saint due to their existing obligations or circumstances.

Olivia, if anyone from your office takes Saint home with them, I would like your help to visit their home and assess for yourself whether he has been well taken care of. If you certify he is so, then and only then, should you reveal the details about my property and money, that I want to give it to them.

I had my home registered to my name after George passed away and a little over one hundred thousand dollars in my bank account. All these should be transferred to the kind person who looks after Saint.

Thank You.

With love and affection,

Madeline Kemp."

Elias, Hannah, and Liam are speechless for a while. Olivia breaks the silence.

"And, Elias, I do have the list that Madeline gave me. Here it is; look!"

"It's okay, Olivia. I don't want to know who else is on the list."

"It's alright, really. See for yourself. Please." Olivia hands him the list. Elias hesitantly takes it.

Elias looks at the list on a sheet of paper and finds only one name that is not canceled. "Elias Smith." All other names were crossed out.

Elias feels overwhelmed.

"Why me??"

Olivia answers. "Good old friend! You know! And even if you don't, Saint does. By the way, Madeline crossed off all the other names, not me."

Olivia hugs Elias and asks, "How many people do you think opted to take care of Saint?"

Elias does not speak. Hannah does. "Is it just Elias who opted?"

Olivia answers. "Yes, Hannah. People like younger dogs, and everyone knows Saint is old. I believe Madeline just knew in her heart that wouldn't matter to Elias."

Olivia leaves. Elias still looks stunned. Hannah affectionately holds her husband's hands.

"Hannah, this is unbelievable! Madeline would have met me only three times I can remember outside of the parties. The first time was with George. The next two times were at her home when I was fixing her car and when she invited me over shortly after."

"Oh! What happened to her car?"

"I went to see her after George died. I sat with her; she didn't say much. I felt she needed someone to be around. I sat with her just as I would with my mother. That's all. And then when I was leaving, I remembered George having trouble with his car the last week.

I mentioned it and asked her if it would be okay to look under the hood. I did some work and made it run. The next day I had the car brought to our office, serviced it further, and sent it home."

"You serviced it?"

"I did. But I didn't tell Madeline about it."

"Did you charge her?"

"No."

"Did your company pay for it?"

"They might have had I asked. I just paid it myself because I wanted to do what I could for Madeline in memory and honor of George. Madeline might have thought of it as a complimentary service from the office. I informed the mechanic to say so if she asked anything about expenses.

I called her a week after. She thanked our office and me for taking care of the car and said it was running smooth as silk after the service."

"Don't overthink, Elias. You know why I married you. We, women, feel who you are. You don't have to say much." Hannah gently presses her hands on Elias' shoulders.

Liam walks to his father and gives him a hug. Liam says he wants to be like him. Elias looks serene and talks to them for a long time before going to bed.

Saint is unusually excited and keeps climbing on Elias all the time. He takes quick laps in the living room, stops, runs to Elias, and keeps repeating his pattern.

Does Saint know what happened here? Is he aware? Who knows?

All three of them are experiencing Saint to be even more excited than he has been so far. This is a fact of their experience. Just as Madeline did, they also believe Saint is extraordinary. However, Saint doesn't seem to care about what anybody thinks about him. Saint cares about Elias and his family, and he seems to be more than content with what he has.

If we are content with what we have, does that mean we won't feel motivated to grow further?

18

Technology, nature's child!

Pat finishes the Skype call with his friends. He's pleased with the progress they're making on their Missing Children initiative. Caring for others and taking supportive actions has become part of his life, for which he feels the same happiness as planting seeds in his garden.

Their initiative has avoided turning into an organization with its own life and demands by not taking a detour from the original objective. Pat has faced many such unfortunate diversions in his life. In all those other organizations, he experienced that the members started to serve the leader's agenda or agendas and gradually became distant from the original cause for which the organization was formed. He appreciates that Naren and his other friends are on the same page. They're sticking to the objective, treating a social cause as an activity of their day-to-day life.

Megan calls him, "Let's go, Gramps. We're already late."

Pat snaps funnily, "Don't call me that! You little puppy!"

Megan laughs nonstop, and Pat joins her laughter. They both run to his truck.

"When am I going to drive your truck?"

"Soon, Meg. Just grow another foot taller, and I'll teach you how to drive."

"Come on, I am already 5 feet tall."

"Well, to drive my truck, one needs to be 6 feet tall." Pat chuckles and gives life to the engine with the turn of the ignition key.

Today is 'Grandpa's day out' with Megan, and Pat has been looking forward to it.

Megan is partly busy with her extracurricular activities on the weekends when Pat visits. He drives a hundred and fifty miles every Friday to see Megan and the rest of the family for the weekend. It's usually group-time, so they planned a day just for themselves a couple of months in advance. It was a challenge to convince the family that they'd go away on Pat's birthday, but somehow Megan succeeded.

"Where are we going, Meg?"

"Gramps! You will follow my directions, and that's all you need to know."

Pat smiles and thinks how nice it is to occasionally give up control to a dear one you trust. It's a pleasant drive where the winter is not yet invited by the trees. It won't be winter for at least another month and a half, allowing us to remember our roots. Aren't our bodies the products of trees and other plant life? They clean the environment and are responsible for the cleanliness of our invisible food – oxygen.

Pat and Megan are driving farther up north, and the scenery is gorgeous. After about fifty miles or so, Megan asks Pat to take the next exit. Megan has her iPhone navigating the way. Pat takes the exit and recognizes that he had been on the side road before, but can't recall which year and where exactly he went off the freeway.

The truck eases through the local streets and finally turns down a dirt road. As soon as they enter, Pat feels the difference in the atmosphere. It's cooler, with more trees than they had seen by the roadside. Beyond the physical comfort the trees render, he also feels a calm presence. Without analyzing much, he enjoys the atmosphere and keeps driving. After about two miles, they begin to see buildings. They are modern and traditional— a total of seven buildings surrounded by lots of trees. No building is more than two stories high.

"What's the matter with number seven and people?"

Pat chuckles as he feels excited about the place and about what he will experience next.

Megan says, "The next stop will be the first building. Happy birthday Gramps."

"Thanks, dear."

Megan takes Pat to the first building. Pat's curiosity greatly increases. It's ten o'clock in the morning, sunny, and the air is so pure. There are lots of parrots, pigeons, peacocks, and cuckoos. Their presence and voices are enchanting.

When Pat enters the doors, he is greeted by a melodious and loud, "Happy birthday to you, Pat."

There are twenty kids and four adults - two women and two men. All are standing in a semicircle, with a table in the center. In the middle of the table is a cake, large enough to serve thirty people. The flavor is coffee and chocolate. Sixty candles are surrounding the cake, each on a stand at the periphery of the table. The table is decorated with many things, including a wooden book and a beautiful block that Pat made for Megan's birthday a year ago. The book-like block has the carving, "The book of life," with a photograph of Megan right above it.

Pat enjoys all the guests, gives Megan a hug, and shares his gratitude for her and everyone. Megan holds his hands and takes him to the table. After he cuts the cake, she hands him a case of books, all by his favorite authors. Megan says they're from all of them. Pat recognizes more than half of the guests. When he visited Megan a few months ago, he went to her school and gave a few classes on woodworking, instructing kids or parents who wanted help. They were all thrilled!

Megan tells Pat that she arranged a camp for a couple of days after discussing the idea with her class and teachers. The four adults are all teachers who agreed to chaperone the kids. The theme of the camp is, "Technology nature's child." Pat asks Megan to clarify what that means.

Megan answers, "The raw materials to make our cellphones are all-natural. Our approach to technology is unnatural, not the technology itself, in most cases."

"What about plastics, which are not bio-degradable?"

"Humans came up with the composition of the plastic. And why did we invent plastic?"

Pat stops himself and asks Megan if they could discuss it later as others are waiting to talk with him. Megan and Pat pause their conversation and spend the next couple of hours meeting and speaking with the others. It's quality time, well spent.

The workshop will start tomorrow. The teachers wanted the kids to interact freely and soak in the atmosphere for a day.

After lunch, Megan and Pat go for a walk. The cool breeze is accompanied by the bright sun. It's a terrific combination.

"Now tell me, Gramps. Why did we come up with plastic?"

"It's cheap and easy to manufacture."

"Is it made of anything that's not from the earth?"

"No."

"Then what makes it not natural?"

"It doesn't decompose and become part of the earth."

"Correct. We didn't consider the importance of such a need when plastic was first manufactured."

"Yes, and we used it in much lower amounts. But now we use it everywhere: Bottles, phone cases, motorcycle parts, and thousands of other things. I could go on and on. Polyethylene carry bags is another example. The earth cannot process our garbage."

"Yes, Gramps. And we blame it on technology instead of our approach. The polyethylene bag is a loyal carrier. Isn't it? It just serves the purpose we designed it for. Sometimes nature is also unfriendly and threatens our lives, as disposed plastic bags threaten the sea life and organisms."

"What do you mean?"

"Hurricanes, tornadoes, volcanoes, wildfire, and floods, all acts of nature, can destroy human lives, animals, and plants."

"That's different. We have a choice."

"We do! I simply meant to say, both technology and nature have different expressions, some expressions that help us and others that don't."

"You're right! We're trying to emulate nature in our tools, like modeling flights after birds, for instance. Unlike nature, meaning raw, unprocessed materials that sustain life, like water, what we make always has some destructive side effect."

"Do all the things we make have destructive effects, Grandpa?" Megan asks with concern.

Pat immediately says, "No! Pots, woodwork from fallen trees…"

Megan interjects, "Only fallen trees?"

Pat says reflectively, "Well, all trees. Wood and clay just become part of the earth. You know, plastic waste alone is not the problem. So many forests were destroyed and are being destroyed as we speak for needless furniture, houses, and buildings."

"Why, Grandpa?"

"We take more than what we need. Human wants and cravings are limitless. Seemingly infinite nature sometimes falls shy of what we can take. We spoke about this earlier too, Megan. We make things for people who can afford them, and we keep on selling things to people."

Megan speaks. "Yes, Grandpa. Most of our population is only capable of using technology, while some are also inventors. We somehow lost the awareness that we have more control over technology than over raw materials in nature. This loss is because most of us are just users who think only about our needs and wants, I guess.

In being only users who just evaluate how attractive what we buy is, and/or how cheap it is, and/or how the product's quality is, we lost the practice to question and think other things about the product. How is it made? Is it produced by exploiting people by underpaying them? Is the natural ecosystem preserved after sourcing the raw materials? And more.

If we follow the path of living and thinking about getting what we want, no matter the expense, we will also face the negative consequence of incomplete technology and its by-products. We will not stop questioning the companies on how they produce, which are a big part of the cause of these problems. We will only consider happiness as the result of buying on our own terms.

In our camp, "Technology is Nature," we want to discuss this one topic, Gramps. How to save the environment for ourselves and our co-habitants, for generations to come!

We've made a product, a cell phone with modular parts. You can easily replace any part and repair it so that you can use the phone for many years. There's a company in Europe that already does this. We have an in-house techie in our class, Eric, who is learning how to build a modular phone. If all things go well, we will release our first home-built phone six months from now. We're also talking to the same European company's suppliers to procure 'conflict and exploit free' raw materials to make the phone. Tomorrow morning Eric will give a demonstration of his work and research. You're going to love it!"

Pat doesn't say a word. He looks at his fourteen-year-old granddaughter with lots of affection and humility in his eyes. He is hopeful and confident in the younger generation, now more than ever.

What will it take to recognize and nurture our kids as tomorrow's leaders?

19

Lingering seeds!

"Have you ever thought how a jungle could have come to be? How did the millions of trees, herbs, shrubs and grass come into existence? How many seeds might have taken for all the trees to come to life? What created the first seed? It's fascinating!"

Kamali is writing in her diary after watching a program on the National Geographic channel. She is preparing for a speech competition at her school. Naren is on the easy chair with his eyes closed. He's thinking deeply about an important topic. Since he was a boy, he loved gadgets. His desire for new gadgets explodes like a mushroom cloud in his mind unless he's careful. It takes a lot of energy, which he can use for his ever-growing list of projects.

Naren feels blessed about Uma's presence in his life. Uma understands his desire and does not judge him. Before marriage, Naren would spend hours researching gadgets, buy the one he likes and then sell it away, feeling guilty that he was wasting money. Thanks to Uma's loving words and understanding, he was finally able to keep a gadget he likes and uses without creating needless guilt.

At the same time, when Uma or his friend asks about a gadget to buy, Naren starts his research and finds himself as if he is buying the gadget for himself and loses his focus on other projects.

Uma doesn't judge why Naren has such a tendency, especially when she is aware he has also meditated for years and is a trainer in meditation. Naren taught her how to meditate. She's able to recognize Naren's strength in both fields, spiritual and material, and nudges him gently to trust himself and his decisions about how to use his time.

As he concludes his meditation and thinking, Naren feels more grateful to Uma. He arrives at an understanding that he has not yet separated his love for gadgets and the attraction he has for them. *He finds that attraction strengthens his will to possess. Love encourages his will to understand the objects of his desire and be happy even if the thing is not in his possession.*

Naren hears Kamali rehearsing as if she is preparing for a speech. He walks to her and says, "I heard you partly, Kamali. Are you going to give a speech?"

"Yes, Dad. I have a school assignment to choose any topic and present it within an hour. I'm fascinated by jungles. So, I'm going to talk about how a jungle might have come into existence, using a slide show I'm putting together. I'm researching the Amazon rainforest to support my speech.

I was amazed when I learned that between 365 and 385 million years ago, plants gave rise to their young through seeds and that they had other ways of doing it before then.

The incredible jungles and forests on our earth are the result of millions of years of evolution. Neat, isn't it?"

"Very neat!" Naren gives a thumbs up to Kamali and walks to the kitchen. Uma greets him and hands him a cup of coffee.

"Someday, I will stop coffee. But I'll always be a fan of your coffee, Uma!"

Uma smiles and asks, "What were you doing?"

"I was meditating and reflecting on a decision. Have you completed the deliverables for your new module?"

"Yes, and on time. I thought we would fail to complete the work on schedule. Kaylee, my Australian team member, did a great job and helped us cross the finish line."

"I forgot what it's like to work towards an aggressive deadline. It's been seven years since I produced in that manner." Naren chuckles.

"Well! Your life is more adventurous than our software deliverables, Naren."

"Haha! So, what time do you want to drive to the city?"

"Two hours from now. Is that good?"

"Yeah."

Naren walks out of his home and strolls in the field. He wants to take a dip in the water tank through which the water from the ground-well flows to the fields.

Enjoying the cool water, he goes to a deep meditative state while being aware of the surroundings. He could hear almost every leaf, the bees' finest hum from a distance, and the consistent sound of the water flowing into the tank and then to the fields.

He asks himself, "Would I trade this experience for some new gadget?" "No," is his response. A few years ago, he would have honestly answered, "Yes." And he asks another question, "Would I trade my time with Uma for a new gadget?" The answer is a resounding 'No.'

After spending an hour in the water, Naren walks home. His emotions have changed, and his thoughts have switched to a more balanced state. He is now thinking about what Kamali shared.

In the jungle, wild weeds grow as fully and easily as the trees and plants, which are useful for people. Nature does not differentiate. We classify the plants based on human needs and wants. As long as the seeds are in the soil, the new growth is a certainty. We don't know when, but somehow, some or many of the seeds will come to life.

Perhaps it's the same with our cravings. As long as the wish remains in our mind, it draws strength from the soil, which is our emotions, and germinate unexpectedly.

Desire is essential to move both spiritually and materially. A desire, when it is motivation, is a movement forward and the motor of human life. Desire, when it's an addiction, creates stagnation and stifles the human spirit. Addiction drowns the intellect in the emotions about the thing one is addicted to. Motivation supplements the intellect with the necessary fuel, emotions, to act.

Love consciously developed by a person helps modify the choice of one's desires – from addiction towards a material thing to motivation towards a principled life.

These conclusions are not new and have been said by many people from time immemorial in different words and ways. The important thing is that Naren arrives at these conclusions for and by himself.

Naren is excited and is walking with a lot of joy. When he arrives home, he finds Uma applying an ointment to the index finger of her left hand. He rushes to her with concern.

"What happened, honey?"

"I accidentally cut my finger while I was slicing the vegetables."

"Ah, oh! Allow me." Naren swiftly takes over from her and applies the ointment. He also places a piece of cotton and puts a band-aid on her finger.

"No big deal, Naren!"

"Yes, yes, no biggie."

"I was just thinking about getting all the papers ready to apply for the travel. I lost myself when I felt worried about not making it on time. That's when I cut my finger."

"I get it. Let me finish the kitchen work." Naren garnishes the curry and transfers the cooked rice from the pressure cooker, then swiftly moves to the sink, cleans all the utensils, and wipes the tabletop.

Uma watches him affectionately.

After dinner, Kamali goes to bed early. She wants to wake up at 5:30 a.m. Uma and Naren go for a walk. Naren holds her hand dearly. They spend a quiet 'thirty-minute-walk,' after which Naren says, "I want to strengthen the desires that move me, not the ones that are an addiction.

"Me too, Naren! Thank you!" Uma speaks slowly and gives him a hug. There was nothing more to explain.

What is, perhaps, the most important quality essential to build a desire that's motivation?

20

Nevets!

It was circa 2013; Naren was preparing to recite a sonnet he wrote. After practicing in front of the mirror at least a dozen times, he turned to Nevets for help. Nevets and Naren lived in the same neighborhood and had attended a few educational seminars together. Nevets' simplicity, which supersedes his brilliance in many fields, including computer programming, singing, and athleticism, moved Naren instantly.

Nevets understood Naren's passion for language and expression immediately in their very first meeting. He was 100% present with Naren and helped Naren to pronounce English correctly whenever there was an opportunity. Naren also trained for a marathon, inspired by Nevets. Naren's sonnet sounded much better when Nevets worked with Naren on the correct pronunciation of just a few words.

"It would be a shame if I didn't help you bring your beautiful writing to life and the way you intended it." These were Nevets' words when Naren went to thank him after the performance.

Naren's constant travel schedule did not allow for them to spend a lot of time together. Despite his busy itinerary, his fondness for Nevets means he always found time to write the occasional note to him over the years he has known him.

When Nevets moved to California, Naren had also relocated to India, putting them almost on opposite sides of the planet. They were each building new ventures of their own and focusing on their families, especially about being with their children. After three years, Naren wrote to Nevets, taking advantage of one of the many social media messaging services, and made a commitment to not have such a long break again. Nevets responded immediately, thus beginning a new phase of their friendship.

Coincidentally, Nevets and Pat also connected shortly after. In one of the conversations, Pat mentioned his meeting Billy in a diner.

Nevets asked, "Pat! I am about to go to New Jersey for a conference followed by a week of meetings at my employer's Princeton office. I want to go to the diner you mentioned. What is its address?"

Nevets was committed to meet Billy after hearing about him from Pat. Pat gave the address and mentioned he would do his best to meet up with him and Billy. It is Pat's busiest time of the year and his best opportunity to make money before winter arrived. His carpentry business is slow in winter, so he engages more in working with people until the Spring. Most of his counseling is public service, for which Pat does not charge any fee.

Neither wanted to miss a chance to meet, so Nevets told Pat he'd plan a trip on the weekend to see him in upstate New York before traveling back to California.

Jenny shares her husband's excitement and bakes two sets of cookies for Pat and his grandkids. When Nevets mentioned Billy, she didn't hesitate to bake extra for the lovely old man about whom she had heard.

"What if Billy is off duty when I'm in Jersey?" Nevets not only thought about it but also asked Pat. Pat laughed aloud. "Hey, buddy! You might not have felt this much excitement to meet your wife! I'm gonna tell Jenny!"

Nevets laughed it off but made sure he called the diner and spoke to the manager on duty to confirm Billy works that week. Nevets could have talked to Billy, but he didn't. He wanted the first meeting to be in person.

Two weeks passed. Nevets is excited as he lands at the Newark airport, and unsurprisingly, he drives the rental car straight to the diner. It's a lovely evening, and his thoughts are adrift along with the clouds.

The diner looks beautiful with the scarlet sky in the background. Nevets finds the sight of the parking area to be refreshing as there are trees evenly planted throughout the lot. There is a name given to each tree. Nevets walks close to find each name to be that of a woman, well known or otherwise.

When he walks from the parking lot, he notices an elderly couple sitting on a bench close to the exit. They've been observing him for a long time.

"Billy planted each tree. He's been waiting at this diner for many decades." Nevets is astonished as they speak, and his respect for Billy keeps growing.

He says, "That's great to know, thanks! You both look lovely. Have a good evening."

As soon as Nevets enters the diner, he looks for Billy, and he finds him serving a family. He asks the man at the cash register to give him a booth in the row Billy serves. The man recognizes Nevets' voice.

"You just called me from the airport, didn't you? And you're the one who called a couple of weeks ago from California."

"Yes, sir. I'm Nevets."

"I've never heard the name Nevets in my life. I'm Tom." The man chuckles as he walks with Nevets to a booth.

"Billy! Your reputation travels all over America. Here is Nevets from California. He's the one who called and asked if you'd be working this week."

Billy looks at Nevets affectionately and says, "Hello Steven! How do you do?" His eyes twinkle as he smiles.

Nevets laughs while Tom tells Billy, "His name is Nevets. Maybe you didn't hear me well."

"Fortunately, I still have good hearing, young man! Perhaps you didn't hear the name well."

And Nevets hands his driver's license to Tom to have a look. The name on the ID is Steven Wilson.

"S T E V E N," Tom spells each word and blushes.

"Oh! I see. Okay! You two have fun talking! Thank you, Steven. And Billy, take good care of our guest. He has come a long way." Tom smiles warmly.

"What can I get you, Nevets?" Billy asks gently.

"I would love a stack of blueberry pancakes with a side of toast and home fries, and it will be great if you could sit and chat with me a bit, Billy. Would that be possible?"

Tom says, "It's always possible. We're happy when Billy talks to our customers. I actually feel that it's Billy who brings us the business as his friends and clients come here to meet him.

Billy thanks Tom and says, "Don't say that, Tommy boy! You, the diner and its staff, and all our customers truly give me a home and a purpose."

Billy turns to Nevets, "I'm grateful to sit with you, Mr. Nevets. But only after I bring your food. Thank you."

Billy walks swiftly, and Nevets ponders whether he could ask people to call him Steven. His classmate Steven Smith was so smart that he aced all the subjects until sixth grade. Nevets struggled all those years and was last in the class.

It was just one unfortunate incident when a joyless teacher mocked him, saying he was the reverse of the bright and talented Steven (Smith), so the teacher started calling him Nevets. Since that event, he was called Nevets by most of his classmates. He studied in a public school in a county in New York known for extreme bullying.

As Nevets had trouble at the school, he continued being quiet and spending as much time as possible alone in his home. Usually, when he was home, he played video games on his dad's computer. His dad, a great programmer, was in love with computers and had two at home. He frequently encouraged Nevets to use the computer. Sometimes he noticed and asked Nevets to refrain from playing games but mostly left Nevets on his own.

It was the early days of gaming on computers that would be called ancient by today's kids. Nevets' mom, Lily, is a doctor who truly cared for and about people and dedicated time outside of her regular duty at the hospital for the general public. She helped people who couldn't afford the cost of treatments or insurance, or prescriptions.

Lily would sometimes pay for her patients from her own pocket. She also created regular fundraisers for their care.

Lily understood that Nevets needed care, but her ideas of how to nurture and provide for him differed from other moms. She often took Nevets along with her to meet ailing people at their homes. Lily is exceptionally social, and she helped Nevets interact with people so he could learn about their pains and triumphs. She would not hesitate to introduce Nevets to the kids of the families she provided medical care to. She thought having her son experience compassion, kindness and playfulness would be perfect antidotes for being bullied at school.

Lily always attended the school's planned parent-teacher conferences and one on one meetings with his teachers. She always believed Nevets would learn a great deal from the unfriendly environment about life and become a fine young man. However, Lily could not find a way to help him study well. She didn't give up and took Nevets to doctors, counselors, and psychologists. Lily also refused to move out of town to change school, believing he could succeed anywhere if he survived this environment. It proved to be true in the years to come.

A loving woman and math teacher named Margaret came to Nevets' rescue when she moved to town. Margaret quickly understood the way Nevets processed information was different from most kids.

Margaret figured that Nevets performed all his computations and wrote things mentally as if there was an invisible board in front of him. She studied Nevets intensely for weeks to arrive at that conclusion. One day she asked the class to do a difficult computation on paper, multiplication of large numbers. As usual, Nevets struggled to complete the calculation. The kids laughed at him. Margaret did not punish them. Instead, she gave a new challenge.

"Everybody listen! Now I want you to multiply 34986 by 59685, but without your pencil and notebook. You can't write on the wall or anywhere. If you want, you can write in the air."

Some kids looked in disbelief and didn't even attempt it. Some others tried and gave all the wrong answers, feeling lost in the middle. Nevets was quiet, and Margaret asked him if he could share the answer aloud.

Nevets did, and Margaret made sure everyone listened to his answer. Then Margaret called for Steven Smith and had him perform the calculation on the blackboard. The answer matched Nevets'.

Steven Smith clapped nonstop, looking at Nevets. Margaret threw a few more long computations and had the entire class watch as Nevets perform Mathematics in the air. Nevets looked like a maestro composing music, who would beautifully conduct his hands, engaging his orchestra to produce sounds unheard of and astonishing.

He completed each of the calculations that Margaret assigned him in record time. His classmates, even the usual rude ones, applauded. The event became unforgettable in the history of the school. Everyone talked about it for months and would ask Nevets to perform complex mathematics in the air. And he would, cheerfully.

One day Margaret asked the class, "Is our Steven still to be called Nevets because he is stupid?"

Most of the kids screamed, "No." There were a few who unfortunately turned joyless and said, "Yes." Steven Smith said, "He is Nevets because there is no Steven like him. He is awesome." Steven Smith never bullied Steven Wilson or called him Nevets. He always called Steven Wilson "Steve," although one could count the number of times Steven Smith called anyone by their name. Steven Smith did not speak much, and mostly he kept to himself and his studies. Somehow Nevets' display of brilliance orchestrated by a dedicated teacher opened Steven's heart. And he started being social, first with Nevets and then with the rest of the class.

People, kids, and teachers alike still referred to Steven Wilson as Nevets as they got so used to it at the school. Lily always called him 'my dear,' where his father called him 'buddy boy.' Steven Wilson kept the nickname Nevets and continued to introduce himself that way over time, as he also got used to it.

Margaret explained to all the other teachers what she observed with Steve. She had them conduct examinations and verbal tests for Nevets. Margaret was at first shocked how no one noticed or cared about Nevets' challenge. Lily knew this limitation and had asked the school many times to conduct oral examinations.

Even so, the teachers wouldn't listen to her. They told her that in return for all the service Lily was doing for the community, they would simply pass Nevets to subsequent grades each year. That is all they could do. Lily was confident and persistent in her effort that she could find a way to help Nevets write.

Eventually, Margaret found a method to help Nevets' writing ability by consulting educators who worked with challenged children. In two years, Nevets was able to write very well. Since the teachers had oral examinations for Nevets, he aced all his subjects, and Steven Smith came second in class. Nevets, a Steven like no other, was grateful for Margaret and for the friendship with Steven Smith.

In two years, Steven Smith moved along with his family to California, and Nevets missed getting together with a true friend. As time passed, the physical distance grew to other spaces as well, and Nevets didn't hear from his buddy. Nevets remained in touch with the lovely Margaret, who is in her eighties now. He visits her at least once a year. He keeps searching for Steven Smith and hopes to find him.

Nevets shared the whole story with Billy in response to his question on how he really likes to be called Nevets.

"I think perhaps you want to be called 'Steve'," Billy said.

"Yes, Billy. Somehow in your presence, I remembered all about my school life more vividly than ever and about Steven."

"That was a wonderful teacher and a wonderful kid." Billy is referring to Margaret and Steven Smith. "We need all the teachers to be like Margaret. Unfortunately, many teachers and parents do not understand the concept of punishment and reward very well."

Steve almost jumps up from his seat and says, "That is exactly what I've been bothered about and have been discussing with my wife, Jenny."

Billy smiles and speaks further. "We try our best to mimic nature. But we fail because we are all not as accepting as nature is. When accepting everyone 'as is' becomes as natural as breathing, so much so that the concept of acceptance itself is gone, we will know how to act like nature - with our children and within ourselves - easily correcting our mistakes.

Instead, we punish our children and each other hoping they/we will learn. We want them to learn about the losses or damage caused by their mistakes. And we think yelling or beating or some random time-outs is the solution to help kids understand the value of something. We end up creating a new behavior in them that they either fear and comply with us because we punish, or they resist and defy us.

Almost everyone in the world does this. Thus, we understand the holistic nature of everything in the world, including people, a near-impossible comprehension. When someone fears or acts out of anger with another, how can they comprehend the value the other person is trying to protect.

I watched a neighbor yelling at another neighbor's kid because the kid broke a window while playing baseball. The kid was terrified. Would the kid understand the window's value, the hard labor behind its creation, the evolution of manufacturing practices for hundreds of years, if not thousands, that created the window in the house? Even if he did, what was present in his mind and heart? Was it the fear of getting yelled at, kicked, or was it the feelings of magnificence about the origin, existence, and value of the window and the pain of breaking it?"

Steve understands the limitations in society very well. What Billy says is an elementary fact, a truth that everyone perhaps already knows or comprehends. However, we still enact the behaviors of yelling, beating, or doing some form of inflicting harm to change a person and, in some worst cases, only as revenge. He voices this concern to Billy.

"I understand. Knowing or being able to know is one thing. Acting solemnly on what we know is another level altogether. It's not complex. It just requires a sincere commitment and desire to apply our will against what our emotion-soaked thoughts cry for."

"Emotion-soaked thoughts?" Steve looks at Billy curiously.

"Yes. If I ask you what this is, you will say it is "Letter A," somewhat neutrally, right?" Billy was pointing his finger to a large "A" printed on the menu.

"I would, and definitely with a neutral inflection in my voice. I'm not traumatized by the letter, 'A,'" Steve chuckles.

"Correct! Therein lies the precious thing in your statement, 'traumatized.' A thought becomes so powerful that it could be compulsive, pushing us to act, even against our wisdom, when emotions are intensely associated with the thought. In those cases, our wisdom, or any knowledge we have about the subject, simply becomes like the thought of the letter 'A,' less emotionally charged or even neutral. The emotion-soaked ideas win."

"True." Steve understands clearly.

"So, the ability to pause despite the storm of emotions dancing wildly in our heart becomes paramount. You know, I'm a fan of two lovely and humble souls, Viktor Frankl and Jiddu Krishnamurti. I learned most of what I know from them and observing life. Viktor Frankl spoke in simple words about stimulus and response and the space in between them. When we are able to stay in that space, we can alter our responses for the progress of all."

"Progress of all, hmm!"

"Yes, it's not always the one being instructed or informed who is learning something new about themselves, but it's also the speaker about kindness and teamwork. How can these two exist without each other? And how can humanity survive without teamwork?"

Steve sits still for a moment, reflecting on the chaos that exists in his multicultural team. The chaos peaks when there's a change in the team, especially when someone leaves and a new person or people join. When he shares that, Billy reflects for a moment.

"The new person is might be worried about their own potential failure and losses. Moreover, they might be worried whether the other team members would approve of them and whether their boss, the leader, would accept them, etc. If you help them understand you, and the rest of the old team also expresses those fears and worries about them, the new person may feel relaxed and perhaps will care about the team. They will not feel alone."

"What?" Steve never thought of doing such a thing. He is kind and compassionate but has not explored this new boundary of vulnerability.

"In the men's world, we want to appear strong. Even the friendliest person has this complex. Especially when you are in a position of authority or power, you keep limits. Some limits are necessary so that the team looks up to you. And you decide when to loosen, and when not."

Steve is astonished. Billy's unspoken tenderness, affection, and love touch him more than his words. Steve asks where else Billy worked before joining the diner.

Billy says, "I always worked here. My salary plus tips pay as well as many other well-paid jobs, and I enjoy meeting people. A few years ago, after going home, I taught the kids in the neighborhood what I know about language, science, and mathematics. Now I just go home and read. If anyone wants to talk, my door is always open. And there is always someone."

Steve asks if he can have Billy's phone number. Billy writes his number on a piece of paper and says he only uses a landline. Steve is not surprised.

"Billy, if you don't mind me asking, don't you have any family living with you?"

"Well! Marlie and I lived for more than six decades at our home. She left me two years ago. I live alone now, but my home is filled on the weekend with all my grandchildren and great-grandchildren visiting me. They don't miss seeing me on the weekends, no matter what."

"I'm so happy to hear that, Billy. I am going to see Pat this weekend. It is Pat who told me about you."

They continue taking for another three hours, after which they both are served a meal. Tom tells them that it's on the house and a special dish that is not on the menu. Steve and Billy thank Tom and enjoy an extended conversation over their dinner.

When they're done eating, Steve looks at his watch. It's 10 p.m. Billy didn't drive to work today. When Tom says he'll ask one of the team members to drive Billy home, Steve offers to do so.

"Steve, you're not here with your family. Why don't you sleepover at my home tonight and drive to your conference tomorrow?"

Steve didn't expect the offer from Billy. He gladly agrees, and they both walk towards the parking lot.

"Did you give all the trees a female name because the trees are similar to our mothers? They sustain human life, and our body is built over the years consuming plant products," Steve asks Billy.

"That's a good comparison. I named the trees so because I thought if anyone in the future wants to destroy them, the person might, at the very least, hesitate to hurt a woman. And in a best-case scenario, they would honor the tree as he would a woman."

Steve stands still for a moment, stunned at Billy's reply. Billy smiles and puts his right hand on Steve's shoulder, and they gently walk along to the car as a reunited father and son would.

What is the purpose of our lives?

21

Jungle!

"Hello – my name is Kamali. When I was given an opportunity to speak today, I first decided to speak about jungles. I did quite a bit of research and built a slide show, only to abandon the project after three days of extensive work. Why did I abandon the project? It's primarily the fault of my mother and father."

The students, teachers, and parents attending this delectable speech competition are curious and drawn in to what Kamali is going to say next. Naren and Uma are also intrigued.

"I have heard that people go to a temple to feel peace, relaxed, and rejuvenated in the beautiful atmosphere of the synagogue. Sometimes we spend time and meet up with our friends to play, roll in the grass, do pillow fights, and laugh together as we understand each other well. Other times maybe we like our pets more than anything else as they don't judge and just want to see us, be with us.

Have any of you had these experiences? Please raise your hands if you have."

The majority of the audience raise their hands.

Kamali continues.

"That's great. I'm glad so many of you have had these experiences. A few years ago, my father, mother and I went to a hotel. I asked for my favorite food. While eating, my father asked me about my music lessons. I first shared some things about my classes. He listened very attentively. After some time passed, I corrected what I said. I mentioned how long I had been learning to sing choir vs. learning to just sing itself.

He turned to my mother and said, "Kamali is committed to precision." I first understood that as praise.

After several years, I started to see how my father points out the best traits I bring to the table, immediately but subtly, be it in the middle of a conversation, a game, or other activity.

If you were a fish in the water, you wouldn't know how good you were at swimming. But why would a fish need to be told how good it was about that? Is it flattery? Would it not get to its head?

Whether we like it or not, we are born in a world where we like another person for their qualities.

When we are in school, it's, "How beautiful they look! How talented they are! What excellent grades! They're so athletic! Etc." Then, I learned from my parents that when we're out of school in the job market, we like people who possess a unique skill, or one who has more money and wealth, or their attire is amazing, and so on.

Sometimes we also harbor dislike in parallel with our growing admirations. This occurs when we don't have special traits and abilities, or when we're not up to the best, or better than the best, in comparison to others. At the same time, in our families and schools, we learn that it's good to be kind, respectful, and polite.

When you are asked, or it is demanded that you be kind or polite or respectful, how do you feel? Especially when you're two or three years old, do you even understand what those things mean? You may be shocked to know that they get upset in some families if their kids do not sit straight when the elders walk by. They even hit the child. If that is done to you, do you really learn to be kind? Do you really learn to be respectful when you are poorly treated?

My father and mother help me understand what qualities and traits are. He helps me create a balanced personality of skill, values, and love for life.

My father points out things to me I didn't even know. As children, we learn just about anything that interests us. When someone helps me see what I had demonstrated, like when my father commented on my precision, my understanding of the importance of precision grows. I also comprehend more deeply why that's important to me.

In this manner, my parents have pointed out many of my positive traits, as well as my bad ones, and very gently. When dad points out something that I need to change, he first explains how he had done it in his life, including how it made life difficult for himself and others.

He's mindful of how I feel and understands when feedback is too much for me to bear, so he will sometimes drop it till a more appropriate time when he knows I'll be receptive to what he wants to tell me. I'm sure for my sake that he does his homework on how to say it well.

I cannot count the number of days my mother fed me with her own hands or the number of times she came to pick me up after my dance and singing lessons. Her only objective is to see me shine and give me all the things she did or could not have. When I do not listen to what is necessary, she fearlessly and firmly corrects me. Mom is very raw; we are each the reason for our tears, anger, and above all, our love.

I want to share a few memorable moments from my countless collection; most of them are with people. My best friend Akila is here and can vouch for them as she has been to my home many times, and I have often been to her home as well.

My father is not a cook from years of practice but is a cook who became so out of love for us. He ventures into multiple cuisines, whether he knows or not. He has traveled and experienced a lot. And he understands my palette very well. One day, I came home with Akila. I was surprised that there was no difference between how he treated us. He sees her also as a daughter.

Rather than assuming or not caring, he first checked with Akila about the amount of spice she could handle in her food, or if she was allergic to anything. Then he surprised us with an incredibly yummy grill cheese Indian masala sandwich using ciabatta bread. Akila always rates his cooking A+.

My father eagerly watches what I watch and learns to love what I do. By comparison, sometimes I'll play with someone five or six years younger than me and feel out of place, and I also don't always have the same interest when interacting with my peers.

But my father can shift his attitude and state, and become as young as I am when he watches a program with me or when we play and interact.

Sometimes I call him doggy, Chewie (from Star Wars), or puppy and whatnot. He's never gotten upset when I tease him that way.

One day my father got angry with someone who honked at him. The next day while writing in his journal and reflecting on the situation, he admitted his own driving mistakes. He told us that he didn't care for everyone on the road as he did for my mother and me and wanted to change that attitude. And he surely did improve. Since then, when others make mistakes on the road, I no longer see him lose his cool and don't believe he ever will again.

One of the best things I like about him is that he is imperfect and doesn't hesitate to admit or show that he doesn't know something. He strives hard to achieve perfection in his crafts, like cooking. Because of his example, I feel encouraged and can run free without making my desire for perfection my prison.

The things I've told you are some tiny examples of his love. There are some which I won't share. They are my treasure trove, but perhaps I will share them as I become older.

My mother has spent most of her time in India. She is a devotee of 'Devi,' - Parvati, and I have known Devi through her. She is my Devi. I could criticize her or find fault with her to any extent. She never bothers my criticisms much. She loves me dearly, and I couldn't sleep away from her for many, many years, as her presence nourishes me even when I am unconscious, sleeping. She forgets my misdeeds, my mistakes, and has me always in her mind.

One of my favorite things to do with her is traveling. She loves to travel and does not hesitate to take me with her anywhere, whether it's one of her office parties or picnics or vacations to other countries. My mom, like my dad, gives extraordinary care regarding how I develop into a balanced person.

While my father cares about how I relate with others and myself, my mother has given me, among other things, an experiential understanding of how I should handle money.

From an early age, I've been learning and practicing self-discipline to restrict my wishes when it comes to buying anything I want. My mother happily shares with everyone that I'm a kid who can be satisfied with a book and nothing else for days. The is true because of my mother's care, guidance and inspiration.

She taught me how to read. It took me almost six months to develop an interest in reading a new genre of books in English. I was reluctant, but she never gave up. She was patient. She was persistent. She's so happy to share with others how well I read and that I read hundreds of pages in a day. But she never told anyone about how she brought me up to that point - how she instilled in me a deep love for reading.

She introduced discipline in my life by taking me to dance and singing lessons starting from an early age. There were times I did not want to practice, and we would have a temporary and fake fallout. Even when I'm pretending or having a temporary fight with her, she is there in my heart of hearts. I feel nothing but love, affection, and an eternal sweet presence of her.

Many of you have told me how sweet I am. All I can say about that is that you would need to share those compliments with my mother and father.

Nobody knows exactly how all the jungle species have come to be or how the millions of plants and animals have come into existence! Many seeds remain as seeds in the jungle. We don't know if and when they will ever become plants. And we can't tell which ones will be beautiful or which will be wild by looking at the seeds. But the mother earth embraces them all anyway. Such a jungle is my home.

I have heard that people go to the temple to feel peace. They want to feel relaxed and rejuvenated in the beautiful atmosphere of the temple. We go with our friends, play, roll in the grass, have pillow fights, and laugh together as we understand each other well. Sometimes we like our pets more than anything else as they don't judge us and just want to see and be with us. I don't need to do any of that.

My home is that temple. My parents are my friends. They're also like my pets, as I'm like their pet.

Now tell me, is it my fault that I gave up speaking about the jungle? It is entirely my parents' fault that they are such a good dad and mom.

Join me in holding my parents accountable for derailing the subject of my speech. They are here."

Kamali points to Uma and Naren, who are stunned and overjoyed. They could not see everything clearly as their joy is overflowing with tears. Everyone, students and teachers turn to Uma and Naren and give a standing ovation.

Kamali runs from the stage to her father and mother. She hugs them, kisses them, and expresses a million thanks without saying a word.

Kamraj Sundram

Author

Kamraj Sundram identifies himself as fundamentally an artist committed to the deeper meanings and crafts of acting, writing, and speaking. He also is a meditator and a certified meditation trainer. Intrigued by the book of Buddha that his beloved aunt Kalyani introduced to him when he was five, he has walked with a fundamental question.

'What is the purpose of life if we are to die?'

Keeping this question alive, he ventured through various landscapes of life that started from an unheard village in the south of India.

Born in a lower-middle-class family in India, he was committed to raising his family's economic standards and chose engineering for his professional degree.

Kamraj Sundram earned an opportunity to work in the US and other countries, thanks to India's beloved tech company, Infosys.

He has written several essays, articles, and poetry and has also won accolades for his public speaking and plays, since his early teens, in India.

While pursuing a corporate career in the US and a transition to entrepreneurship, he has kept his artistic bent alive by continuing to write and participating in events involving poetry, plays, and dance performances.

His keen interest in self-development led to deep relationships with loving people from different countries both in and outside his work. Such experiences taught him how humanity is the basis of all achievements and offered him a clarity that one can know oneself best by relating with others. He has helped and been helped by numerous like-minded people through coaching and mentoring throughout his adult life.

Collecting and drawing upon all his experiences, Kamraj Sundram is building Sarvah League, a humble endeavor to bringing meaningful films and literary work for the readers and viewers.

Kamraj Sundram is grateful to his family for being his foundation and guiding grace to refine his raw existence, transforming his aggressive competitive spirit into that of cooperation and inspiration, growing along with the other, and above all, with love. He lives in India with his wife and daughter and enjoys a beautiful and meaningful relationship with them. Their loving presence and care inspire his work, including this book.

Steven Ose

Editor

Born and raised in Poughkeepsie, NY, Steven Ose was raised with the family values of a strong Italian mother and French-German father. Like most children, Steven often disagreed with the rules and expectations of his parents and found solace with his grandparents. In their eyes, he was a smart, caring and joyful presence who could do no wrong.

From them, he came to experience unconditional love and what it looked like to treat others with respect and dignity. Would that we all could have had grandparents like his.

Grade school was emotionally and academically challenging for Steven, as he did not thrive in the regimented, one-size-fits-all environment. He excelled in math and computer science, showing promise at the end of senior year for a career in technology. From high school to his mid-20s, he tried myriad jobs before beginning his professional path in information technology. Over 30 years later, he is still actively learning and producing in the IT field.

He found a joy in writing at an early age but considered it a hobby and is new to professional editing. He considers himself of moderate ability, though his clients enjoy the humor and intuition he brings to their work. His goal is to uphold in writing what sounds good when spoken aloud. This is especially useful when a work has been translated to English.

Steven lives in Austin, TX with his wife and younger son. His older son lives in upstate New York. Steven enjoys a strong relationship with both sons and likes to joke that he made all his mistakes on his first one. He knows that one of the most important (and often difficult) relationships to work on is the one with himself.

Made in the USA
Las Vegas, NV
24 December 2021

39304410R10111